MR. FEBRUARY

HEROES OF ROGUE VALLEY: CALENDAR
GUYS
BOOK 2

ANN ROTH

Published by Oliver-Heber Books

0 9 8 7 6 5 4 3 2 1

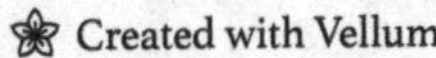 Created with Vellum

INTRODUCTION

Welcome to Ann Roth's exciting new series, Heroes of Rogue Valley: Calendar Guys series. Twelve months, 12 gorgeous firefighter heroes and the women who steal into their hearts and forever change their lives.

Meet Mr. February:

Rafe Donato is a senior firefighter well aware that loving a woman can destroy a man. He will never trust any female with his heart. Jillian Metzger is a talented potter whose biological clock is ticking. Ready to fall in love, get married and start a family, Jillian wants what Rafe cannot give.

Mr. February—Rafe Donato
    Age 32, 6'1" tall, 190 pounds
    Single
    Proud Senior Firefighter
    Time with Guff's Lake Fire Department: 11 years

1

"Come back here, Pooh!" Jillian Metzger shouted as she sprinted across the uneven field adjacent to the cottage.

The Border collie had the gall to bark joyfully and skip over rocks and tree roots at a clip Jillian couldn't begin to keep up with.

To make matters worse, it started to rain. She hadn't taken the time to grab an umbrella, let alone a jacket—she'd simply darted out of the studio in hot pursuit. Not wise, considering temperatures in early March in Rogue Valley tended to be on the south side of chilly.

If and when she managed to catch Pooh, she was going to let her freeloading brother have it. Why couldn't JR keep an eye on his own dog? Because he'd gone out with Chelsea, frittering his day away when he should have been looking for a job.

Pooh was a good fifty yards ahead now, and Jillian quickly losing steam. She was on the verge of collapsing in exhaustion when the dog finally skidded to a stop. Tail wagging, Pooh changed course, trotting toward a man and woman standing slightly uphill, under a big umbrella. What were they doing here in the boonies on a rainy Wednesday morning?

Jillian lurched to a halt to catch her breath and pull herself together before they noticed her. A futile effort, given that she was a sodden mess. Leaning against the trunk of a lofty tree heavy with leaf buds, she tucked her dripping hair behind her ears with icy fingers.

She couldn't tear her gaze from them. What a striking couple. The dark-haired male, muscled and at least six feet tall, wore jeans, a light-blue sports shirt, and a black windbreaker that hugged his broad shoulders. His companion, with her shiny, stylish haircut and designer suit, stood close beside him under the umbrella.

Something about the guy seemed vaguely familiar, but before Jillian could place him, Pooh did the unthinkable—raced forward, jumped up, and planted her muddy paws on his powerful thigh.

"Get down, Pooh!" Jillian cried, pushing away from the trees and running again.

The big man didn't seem all that upset. He patted the dog and then brushed the mud off his jeans, which were neatly pressed, as was his shirt. Clutching the umbrella in both hands, his horrified companion quickly stepped out of reach.

The second his dark gaze met Jillian's, she recognized him. What red-blooded woman could forget those mesmerizing eyes, the strong jaw, and the slight hollows of his cheeks? She was about to come face-to-face with Rafe Donato, aka Mr. February in the Guff's Lake Fire Department calendar.

The calendar, part of the ongoing fund-raising drive for the department's benefit fund, had been released right before Christmas and featured twelve of the most gorgeous firefighters...

Drop-dead, movie-star-handsome Rafe looked even better in person than his photo—if that was even possible. Jillian's heart lifted in an appreciative sigh.

The calendar included certain important facts about each firefighter, stats any woman with a pulse would want to know. According to the details Jillian recalled—and with a calendar hanging on the wall in her studio, she was quite familiar with them—Rafe was single. At least he had been when the calendar was printed. By the intimate look from his lady friend, his status had changed.

"I'm sorry about Pooh," she apologized. "She's supposed to stay in the yard. Instead, the little scamp dug under the fence and lit out."

When Pooh had made her escape, Jillian had been in her pottery studio, creating pieces for one of her retail customers and for the Rogue Valley Arts Festival, which was in March. If she hadn't decided to stretch her back and wander to the window, she wouldn't have noticed until the dog was long gone.

"My dog used to do the same thing."

Rafe flashed a smile, revealing dimples—holy cow, dimples—and extended his arm.

"Rafe Donato."

Wishing she'd dressed in something other than

raggedy work clothes, Jillian wiped her palms on her threadbare, damp jeans before she shook his huge hand. His firm, warm grip engulfed her cold fingers, and his chocolate-brown eyes fixed intently on her.

Her knees wobbled. She glanced away. As attractive as Rafe was, she refused to go all weak and fluttery. He was already taken.

Even if he hadn't been, the ramrod straight posture, military-short hair, meticulously pressed shirt and jeans, and polished black boots screamed order and control. This was the kind of man who made life miserable for everyone around him. At eighteen, she'd left home to get away from that. She would never go back.

Pooh licked Jillian's hand. "Bad girl," she said, but the dog's innocent expression was hard to resist.

Rafe's girlfriend cleared her throat. "I'm Sonia Kaye, Rafe's architect." She started to extend her hand, but, after giving Jillian a quick once-over, offered her card and a perfunctory smile instead. "I should go, Rafe. I've seen enough for now, and I took plenty of photos. I'll be in touch."

"Let me walk you to your car." He held up a finger, signaling Jillian to wait.

Pooh wanted to follow the couple, but Jillian caught hold of her collar. "You're not going anywhere." The dog put wet-dog smell on a whole new level, and Jillian grimaced. "You need a bath."

With JR and Chelsea out, who knew where—they certainly hadn't said good-bye or left a note, but then, they never did—she would likely be the one doing the honors.

Rafe and his architect girlfriend moved in tandem up a gently sloping hill, toward the two expensive sedans parked on a dirt patch some distance away—one, a silver Mercedes, the other a gleaming navy convertible BMW.

Which belonged to him? The sleek BMW, Jillian guessed. It looked cleaner and somehow suited him.

Yep, the convertible was his. Rafe held the umbrella over Sonia's head while she climbed into a silver Mercedes. After flashing a flirty smile, she drove away, her tires churning up mud.

Rafe tromped back to Jillian. "Where do you and Pooh live?"

"Not far. On the other side of the field."

He nodded. "Cy Jackson's property."

"How do you know the name of my landlord?"

"I just bought the two-acre plot you're standing on, and I know everything about this area. Your cottage isn't more than a third of a mile from here, an easy walk, but this driving rain can make even a short distance seem like a long way. How about a lift?"

The offer surprised her. "We couldn't possibly. We're both wet and muddy, and Pooh stinks something terrible." She held her nose.

Rafe didn't argue with her. "You don't even have an umbrella. I do. I also happen to have a spare leash in the trunk of my car. Let me grab it, and I'll walk you and Pooh home."

~

JILLIAN WAS TALL, the top of her head almost level with Rafe's nose. That put her at about five-foot-ten. Long-limbed and slender, she could pass for a runway model—at least from what Rafe imagined. In baggy, wet clothes and dirty sneakers, he couldn't tell.

Her wet, shoulder-length blonde hair lay plastered to her head. Rafe remembered how cold her hand had felt in his. Any minute, her teeth would start to chatter.

"Here," he said, setting the umbrella down to shrug out of his lined windbreaker. "Put this on."

"But I'm a dirty mess."

"You're also freezing cold." He helped her into it then picked up the umbrella and held it over them. "Don't worry, it's washable. Zip up."

She did. The thing swam on her, which was kind of cute.

"How long have you lived on Cy's property?" he asked.

"For almost a year. Last month, I signed a lease for another year."

"We'll be neighbors, then—once I get my house built."

When not at the Guff's Lake Fire Department, Rafe spent his time managing his rental properties. He also kept an eye out for fixer-uppers, which he enjoyed remodeling and selling. With the combined income he earned, he'd finally saved enough to build his dream home without emptying his bank account.

"Your own custom place? Lucky you. Sonia must be so excited."

"Because I hired her to design the house?"

"That and because you're a couple."

He laughed. "We're not together."

"Oh." Jillian looked surprised. "I assumed… You know."

"Getting romantically involved with my architect could be risky."

"Because if it didn't work out, you'd still need her help."

That and because as much as he liked women, and he liked them a lot, he didn't trust a single one enough to live with. Which wasn't quite true—he trusted his paternal grandma and a handful of female teachers from grade school and high school. But he preferred living alone. "Yeah."

Jillian nodded then angled her head. "You're a firefighter, right?"

"You've seen the calendar."

She blushed, adding much-needed color to her pale skin. "I have."

She had a generous mouth and fine, delicate features. "There's something on your chin," he noted, nodding at the gray glob stuck on the underside. The same stuff stained the cuff of her oversize sweatshirt. "And on your sleeve."

She touched the spot on her chin and rubbed at it, laughing self-consciously. "It's clay. I'm a potter."

"Ah. You do that full-time?"

"Yes. I sell to a couple of stores in the area an online. I'm also working on pieces for the Rogue Valley Arts Festival in Medford next month. Until recently, I also taught at the Artist Cooperative on the south side of town."

"You don't teach there anymore?"

"The school closed up shop last month. I'm getting ready to offer classes in my home studio."

"I never figured that little house with room for a studio."

"Actually, I use the outbuilding behind the cottage. With heat, electricity, and a skylight, it's perfect. I think it was originally designed as a workshop for household projects. I got permission from Cy to turn it into my pottery studio. My kiln is behind the building."

Rafe wondered how she made ends meet selling pottery and teaching classes. Having spent the first ten years of his life with his mom, whose sales from herbal concoctions and tie-dye T-shirts had often left them both hungry and moving in a hurry to escape eviction for non-payment of rent, he preferred a steady job with a regular paycheck, and money in the bank.

As they neared the cottage, Pooh woofed and strained at her leash.

"*Now* you want to get home," Jillian quipped. Under her breath, she added, "You'll change your tune when you realize you're about to get a bath."

Rafe chuckled, caught himself, and frowned. He wouldn't let this woman charm him.

Tibetan prayer flags were strung across the eaves over the porch. That and the aging VW van parked behind the hatchback in the gravel driveway reminded him of the years he'd lived with his mom.

Jillian frowned. "It's about time JR got back."

Rafe figured JR was her boyfriend. He wasn't

about to ask—didn't want to know, but the words slipped out. "Who's JR?"

"My brother," she grumbled. "Thanks for walking me home, and for loaning me your jacket."

His unwitting gaze dropped to her plump, inviting lips. Jerking his attention to the jacket, he held out his hand for it.

"Let me clean it first. I'm happy to drop it off at the fire station later."

The guys were sure to razz him. He shrugged. "Sure. I won't be in again until Monday."

"Then you're a part-time firefighter?"

He shook his head. "I work Mondays and Tuesdays, two back-to-back, twenty-four-hour shifts. That's forty-eight hours a week, with five days off in between."

"Your days off sound nice, but isn't it dangerous, working such long hours with no break?"

"We each have a place to bunk at night, so I usually get some sleep. Even on busy nights, I manage all right. After eleven years, I'd better." Ready to leave, he gestured at the cottage. "Stay dry."

He turned away and strode back toward his property.

2

W hen Jillian entered her kitchen through the back door, JR and Chelsea were seated at the little wood table she'd bought at Second Hand Rose, the best shop in town for her budget.

They'd pulled last night's casserole from the fridge and were devouring the leftovers straight from the dish. A casserole Jillian had put together and paid for. She'd planned to reheat those leftovers and serve them for dinner tonight.

Not anymore.

In the month since her twenty-three-year-old brother and his then-five-weeks-pregnant girlfriend had shown up homeless at her door, they'd strained her food budget as well as her patience. As thrilled as Jillian was about becoming an auntie, she had her limits.

She gave JR a dirty look. "You're eating tonight's dinner."

Six years her junior, with a big appetite, he

paused mid-bite and gave a sheepish shrug. "We didn't know you were saving it, Jill."

"I told you last night."

Most of the time, she wanted to throttle him. Still, he was her only sibling, and she loved him dearly. She hadn't laid eyes on him in five years, since he'd left for parts unknown. Then one wintry morning he'd knocked on her door.

As glad as she was to have him back healthy and safe, the years he'd lived on his own hadn't changed him much. As payback for this temporary room and board, while he found a job, saved up, and moved into his own place, he'd agreed to help out whenever she needed him. Occasionally, he followed through, but most of the time he made sure to be gone.

Jillian's patience was rapidly thinning.

Chelsea, barely twenty, raised her eyebrows clear above her dyed-red, shaggy bangs. "You're a wet mess. Does that jacket belong to the guy I saw you with out there? Who is he?"

She *would* notice. "Yes, this is Rafe's jacket. We met when I chased Pooh in the rain." She frowned at JR. "She escaped again."

"Don't look at me." He ran his hand through his equally shaggy, sandy hair. "I penned her in the yard, as you asked. It's not my fault she got out. If someone penned me in, I'd leave, too."

Thanks to their father's rigid rules and harsh forms of discipline, JR had done the same thing the semester before graduating high school.

"Did you say 'Rafe,' Mr. February on the firefighter calendar in your studio?" Chelsea squealed. "Way to go, Jill!"

"He walked me back under his umbrella because I was freezing," Jillian said. "He didn't want me to get even colder and wetter."

JR gave a knowing grin. "But you kept his jacket. I guess you'll be seeing him again."

For some reason irritated, Jillian huffed out a breath. "Will you stop?"

"What's wrong with getting yourself a boyfriend? Since I've been here, you haven't had one."

Until Jillian met the right man, she didn't intend to change that. "Pooh needs a bath, JR."

"In other words, butt out of your love life. Got it. Yeah, I can smell Pooh. When I finish eating, I'll bathe her."

"The sooner, the better. By the way, I told Shannon I'd stop by and see her and Georgia this afternoon. I'll be leaving soon."

Two weeks ago, Jillian's best friend had given birth to Georgia, the sweetest, most perfect infant ever. From the moment Jillian had held her and gazed into her trusting gray eyes, she'd fallen in love. A stunning, aching longing had filled her, for a child of her own. Not sometime in the distant future, but soon. Over the past two weeks, the longing had grown even stronger.

Becoming an auntie would be great, but wouldn't change the fact that in October, a mere seven months from now, Jillian would be thirty.

Her biological clock was ticking, and she was finally ready to settle down with one man and make a life together. Which was pretty amazing, considering a mere two years ago, she hadn't imagined ever wanting kids or marriage. Not even with Douglas, her boyfriend of several years. Jillian had been sure she loved him. And yet, during the months they'd lived together, he'd proposed three times. She'd always turned him down.

Finally, fed up, Douglas had moved out. After Jillian had gotten over the pain of losing him, she'd realized she hadn't really loved him, after all.

Chelsea's eyes lit up. "I'd give anything to see Georgia. Let me go with you, Jill." She bit her lip and glanced at JR. "Unless you need help with Pooh's bath?"

"I can manage. Go ahead, Chels."

Knowing Shannon wouldn't mind, Jillian smiled. "Of course, you can come. But we won't be staying long. Shannon's worn out, and I really need to get back to work. After I shower, change into dry clothes, and grab a bite to eat, we'll leave."

After dinner tonight, she'd run a load of laundry and wash Rafe's jacket. Sometime tomorrow, she would drop it off at the fire station.

And that would be the end of that.

SHANNON GESTURED Jillian and Chelsea into her bungalow with the same dark circles as before under her weary eyes.

Jillian handed her friend the gossip magazine she'd brought. "That's for you to read when you have time. And this is my brother's girlfriend, Chelsea."

Shannon smiled. "I finally get to meet the future mother of Jillian's niece or nephew. Congratulations."

"Thanks." Grinning, Chelsea cupped her barely visible baby bump. "I'm due in September."

While the two women chatted about babies, Jillian excused herself to wash her hands in anticipation of holding Georgia.

"I'm dying to see the baby," Chelsea chirped as Jillian returned. "Where is she?"

Intermittent infant noises punctuated the question, courtesy of the baby monitor on the coffee table.

"Sleeping, but as you can hear, she's just waking up." Shannon gestured in the direction of the nursery. "Do you want to come with me while I get her up and change her?"

"Yes, please," Jillian and Chelsea replied at the same time.

While Shannon deftly diapered the sweet little girl, Jillian marveled at her. "I swear, she's grown in the last two weeks."

"Half an inch and a whole pound," Shannon said proudly.

Chelsea clasped her hands together. "She's so tiny and so cute."

"Would you like to hold her?"

"More than anything."

"Then wash your hands, and we'll see you back in the living room. Here, Jillian, you carry her."

Dying for the honor and still madly in love with

Georgia, Jillian carefully transported the precious bundle to the sofa. "Are you enjoying motherhood?" she asked.

Shannon's smile radiated joy. "I'm exhausted, but I've never loved anyone this much in my life. Except Asher. You should see him with her. He's crazy about her."

"It seems like yesterday you two got married."

"It's only been a year, but when it's right, it's right."

A wave of longing swept through Jillian, for a husband and baby of her own. With a tentative hand, she smoothed Georgia's light-brown hair over her little round head. "Her hair is so soft," she said in wonder. "Don't keel over and die, but I'm admitting here and now that I'm ready to settle down and have a baby, too."

Shannon's eyes widened. "You met someone."

Jillian thought briefly of Rafe, but he was all wrong for her. "Not yet, but I'm ready to start working on that."

"Working on what?" Chelsea asked as she entered the living room.

Giving her head a subtle shake, Jillian warned her friend not to mention what she'd shared. But Shannon's attention had fixed on lifting her child from Jillian's arms, and she didn't notice. "Jillian is ready to fall in love."

Chelsea wore a sly look. "I knew you were interested in Rafe."

"Rafe?" Shannon frowned.

"The guy on the firefighter calendar—Mr. February," Chelsea clarified.

"You know him?" Shannon looked intrigued. "You never said a word."

"You've been kind of busy. Besides, I only met him this morning, when I was out, chasing Pooh," Jillian explained. "He isn't my type."

"A man with his looks is any woman's type," Shannon murmured.

Chelsea nodded. "For an old guy, he's cute."

"Hey, watch it," Jillian said. "He's around the same age as Shannon and me."

Busy making baby talk to Georgia, Chelsea didn't reply. As young as she was, Jillian had a hunch she'd make a good mom.

The baby began to fuss. "She's hungry, and I need to feed her," Shannon said.

Jillian nodded. "And I should get back to the studio."

They all stood. Jillian hugged her friend.

"Good luck with your search for Mr. Right," Shannon murmured in her ear. "Keep me posted."

3

—————

Early Friday morning, Rafe parked off the dirt road a mile or so from where he usually parked when he visited his newest property acquisition.

He exited the car and then leashed Calvin, his sixty-pound Vizsla. In contrast to the previous day, the sky was clear. Despite the chill air, leaf buds on the trees and trills from several hardy birds signaled the coming spring. A great day for a run.

Calvin agreed, and when Hank and Gus, his fellow crewmates, showed up, the dog woofed in excitement. He knew what lay ahead.

Rafe was tight with both men, as well as the other nine firefighters and the captain who worked his shift. Living together every week for forty-eight hours straight meant getting to know each other real well, warts and all. None of them was perfect, but Rafe knew without hesitation that no matter what, they had his back. Just as he had theirs.

After they greeted each other and stretched,

Hank glanced around. "I've never been out here before. It's nice. Which way are we heading?"

An avid runner who'd attended college on a cross-country scholarship, Hank usually set the pace at just short of torture.

Eager to show his buds the site of his future home, Rafe gestured toward the west. "Straight for about a mile then head right. I'll let you know when."

Hank nodded. "You jokers ready?" Without waiting for an answer, he took off at a fast clip.

Rafe was in good shape, but dodging mud and puddles, tree roots, and embedded rocks took its toll. Soon, his breathing grew labored and his leg muscles burned, urging him to slow down.

Not an option. Relying on mindful observation, a tool of self-discipline he'd learned from his father and had honed with years of practice, Rafe concentrated on his breathing and let everything else fall away.

A few yards shy of the turnoff, he lengthened his stride and caught up to Hank. "Turn here."

After veering right, the cross-country fanatic upped his speed to killer level.

Soon they reached the edge of Rafe's property. "This is it," he called out, coming to a stop. Calvin plopped onto the grass, panting. "The site of my new home."

Hands on his knees, Gus gulped air. "Great view of the Siskiyou Mountains," he said when he straightened. "I can see Guff's Lake in the distance, too. Sweet."

The town's namesake was located in the

foothills of the Siskiyou Mountain Range. Snowmelt kept its four-mile diameter waters sparkling and drew locals and tourists for fishing, hiking, and camping. Or for luxury accommodations at the five-star resort and hotel.

Hank wiped sweat off his face with the hem of his T-shirt. "I see why you decided to use this part of your 'vast empire' for yourself. It's about time you did."

Rafe's holdings hadn't exactly reached vast empire status yet, but he approved of the label. "I'm thirty-two," he said. "It's time I built myself a home."

A permanent place, where he could put down roots.

"You hired Sonia to design the house, huh?" Hank asked.

Rafe nodded. "She's the best architect around."

"If she's like the rest of the women you date, she'll probably work for free to get you into the sack, stud."

Ignoring the nickname they used to get a rise out of him, Rafe shook his head. "I admire her work ethic, but otherwise, she's not my type. She has *I'm looking for love and the whole nine yards* written all over her."

Rafe wanted no part of that. His buds understood. They knew what he'd suffered through as a kid, and what a mess he'd been until age ten, when he'd moved in with his dad. Thanks to the man's discipline and structure, Rafe had straightened up.

By the time his dad had married a few years later, Rafe had been on a solid path to success—good grades and a junior varsity position on the middle school basketball team. His stepmom, Lori, had brought her own two kids into the marriage. She hadn't wanted Rafe around. But her acceptance of him had been a deal breaker for Rafe's dad, and she'd learned to tolerate him. Still, she'd never shown him any real warmth, and when she and his dad divorced two years later, the only fallout Rafe had suffered stemmed from his father's grief over the failed marriage.

"I'm about ready for breakfast," he said. "If we go a little farther, we can loop back to where we started. I'll take the lead now."

Hank shrugged. "Go for it."

They were cutting through the woods at a more reasonable pace when Calvin woofed. Bred for hunting, he pointed and strained at his leash. In the distance came an answering bark. Rafe recognized that sharp-pitched sound. Pooh.

He gave Calvin plenty of leash, and moments later, Jillian's cottage, and the woman herself, came into view. Wearing leggings and another long, baggy shirt, hair tucked into a baseball cap, she balanced on a folding ladder, wielding a long-handled paint roller over the weathered green siding of her studio. The new color, purple, was exactly what Rafe would have expected. The same hatchback sat parked in the driveway. He didn't see the ancient van.

"Get a load of those long legs," Hank murmured appreciatively.

Rafe didn't like the way he and Gus looked her over.

"Rafe. Hi," she said, climbing down with a confused smile.

"You know her? Of course you do," Hank murmured. "Introduce us."

Rafe preferred not to, but hell, he wasn't interested in her, so why not? "Jillian, meet Hank and Gus, two of my crewmates. And this is Calvin."

She greeted his dog with pats and friendly murmurs. When she straightened to her full height, the huge firefighters dwarfed her. They each shook her hand.

Suddenly, Calvin pulled hard on his leash. He sized up Pooh, and she did the same. They both growled.

"Easy, boy," Rafe warned in his no-nonsense voice. As soon as his dog obeyed, he allowed the animal to lead the way.

"Pooh looks a lot prettier than she did yesterday," he said. So did Jillian. Not that she'd looked all that bad dripping wet.

"She smells better, too, thanks to a bath. What are you doing out here on a Friday morning?"

"We need to stay in shape," Rafe replied. "And with the weather finally starting to turn nice..." He shrugged. "Plus, I wanted to show these guys where I'll be building my house. I see you're painting your studio."

She nodded. "I decided to brighten up the place before my first class. You should see the gorgeous lime-green paint I got for the trim."

"That purple's bright all by itself."

"What kind of classes?" Gus asked.

"Pottery. I used to teach at the Artist Cooperative, but the school closed, and I decided to teach here. This will be a class for beginners. It starts in two weeks. I have openings, so if you know of anyone who's interested... I printed flyers. Who wants one?"

Both Rafe's crewmates signaled they did. Hank hadn't dated since he'd joined the department two years earlier. He was dealing with some heavy stuff and wasn't ready. But Gus, currently single, looked interested. Rafe barely curtailed a snarl.

Oblivious, Gus grinned at her. "Need help painting?"

"I'll be the one to do that," Rafe volunteered. His own words and gruff tone pulled him up short. What had gotten into him?

"I expected JR to help, but whenever I need a hand, he manages to be gone." She blew out an exasperated breath.

"Watch out for this guy," Gus warned, jerking his thumb Rafe's way. "We call him 'stud' for a reason."

Rafe rolled his eyes. "Don't believe everything either of these fools tell you."

She didn't comment. "Your jacket is in the dryer. I'd planned to drop it by the station, but since you're here... I'll see if it's dry, and grab some flyers for the pottery class."

She disappeared inside.

"Loaning her your jacket—nice move," Hank said.

Gus nodded. "No wonder you're building a house here. Jillian's hot."

That Rafe agreed bothered him. "She's a free spirit," he said.

"Then she probably doesn't want to be tied down any more than you."

Rafe narrow-eyed him. "I wouldn't know, and who the hell cares?"

"It's just an observation," Gus muttered.

"Rafe has a point," Hank said. "Dating her would make for a difficult neighborly relationship after the breakup. Because, sooner or later, he always breaks up with them."

Jillian returned with flyers and jacket, neatly folded. She passed out flyers and then handed Rafe the jacket. "Thanks again for letting me borrow this."

As he took it from her, his fingers brushed hers. Yesterday her skin had been cold. Today she felt warm, nice and warm.

His body took notice and began to stir. Damn. "I need food," he told the guys.

He nodded at Jillian and took off.

THE EXTERIOR of the studio wasn't exactly huge, but Jillian's aching arms thought so. Pushing the paint roller over the siding proved challenging—especially the area above her head.

"Why couldn't you stick around and help, JR, like you promised?" she grumbled.

He and Chelsea had left this morning while she showered, the little sneaks. Jillian had no idea when they would return, but, knowing JR, it would be after she finished the job, probably just in time for dinner.

She couldn't take much more of this.

Her empty stomach growled. As determined as she was to finish painting today, while the weather cooperated, she needed food, and her arms needed a rest. Lunchtime.

Over a sandwich, she thought more about her brother. If he could find a job, he and Chelsea could move out. He wasn't looking very hard, and Jillian was beginning to wonder if he even wanted to work. This worried her. Who would take care of Chelsea and the baby?

Why couldn't he be more responsible? Why couldn't he be more like Rafe? Yes, Rafe was too meticulous and controlled for her tastes, but he had a good job and seemed a genuinely decent guy.

Plus, he was yummy to look at. She let out a dreamy sigh. He and his two equally buff firefighter friends had no business jogging past her house in shorts and tees.

Since the breakup with Douglas, Jillian had dated her share of men uninterested in serious relationships. Until recently, she'd felt the same way.

But now that she wanted a baby, she needed to find a man ready to settle down and start a family. Which meant steering clear of guys like Rafe. Labeled a stud by his own friends.

Jillian didn't expect to see him again, and there was no point in thinking about him.

She finished the sandwich and returned to the great outdoors to resume painting.

She was maneuvering the roller and trying to

hold her shaking arms steady when she heard a car pull up the driveway. The purring engine did not belong to JR's rattling van. Glanced over her shoulder, she noted Rafe's BMW pulling to a stop near her sedan.

He'd come back. As she clambered down the ladder, her wayward heart lifted.

In one smooth, graceful motion, he slid out of his car. Faded jeans hugged his muscular legs, and a faded T-shirt clung to his broad shoulders and flat belly. *Firefighters—Cool under pressure*, the words on the shirt proclaimed. Feeling the opposite of cool, she mentally fanned herself.

He leashed Calvin and let him out of the back seat, which he protected with a terry cloth seat cover. Tail wagging, the dog woofed and made a beeline for Pooh, who appeared to be grinning.

"I never expected to see you again," Jillian said.

He looked surprised. "I said I'd help."

"I didn't realize you meant it." Most of the guys she knew didn't have the time or interest in painting someone else's building.

As badly as she needed help, she wasn't at all sure she wanted Rafe around. He was too darned attractive. "I don't need any help," she assured him. "I'm used to doing things by myself. I'll be fine."

"It'll get done faster with an extra pair of hands. Is it okay to pen Calvin in with Pooh?"

He had a point. She nodded. After Rafe let Calvin into the fenced area, he took the roller from her. "I'll tackle the high-up places, and you do the window trim."

Not about to argue, Jillian stepped into the studio to get the trim brush and the paint.

Working with Rafe wasn't half-bad. He didn't talk much, and neither did she. The lime-green trim looked great with the purple siding and gave the studio the artsy feel Jillian wanted. She needed to replace the income she'd lost when the school at the Artist Cooperative had closed. Teaching pottery classes here would help.

Before long, she needed another break.

"I'm ready to sit down with a cup of tea," she said. "How about you? If you're not a tea drinker, I have pop or coffee."

"Pop sounds good."

"Pop it is."

At the back door, she wiped her feet and waited for him to follow her inside.

4

Jillian had been pretty quiet while Rafe painted with her. Now, while waiting for the water to heat for tea, she still didn't say much. Most women would have chattered away to fill in the awkward silence. Not her.

She seemed comfortable in her own skin, a quality Rafe admired. Who exactly was this woman? He wanted to know. "Tell me about your brother," he said when finally sat down at the kitchen table. "What's 'JR' short for?"

"Junior. His given name is David Gregory Metzger, Junior, after our father. But they're nothing alike."

"Is that good or bad?"

"Both." She gave a pained look. "Dad has always been a strict disciplinarian and difficult to please. Whereas JR drifts around with no sense of responsibility. You'd think now that he's twenty-three, he'd be a responsible adult, but he's still rebelling. He doesn't have a job or any money. That's why he lives with me."

Interesting. Rafe had assumed Jillian's parents were more freewheeling, similar to his mom. "How come your dad is so hard to please? What does he do for a living?"

"He used to be a career army drill sergeant, but now he runs a driver's-ed school up in Seattle. When we were growing up, Dad treated us like recruits. I wanted desperately to please him, and I became the daughter he demanded—the perfect student, the good girl who didn't make any waves. JR went the opposite direction, making bad grades, skipping school, staying out past curfew, and disobeying Dad as often as possible. You can imagine how that went over."

Rafe was getting the picture now.

"Mom wasn't nearly as rigid, and their different ideas about raising us caused a ton of problems. They fought all the time, mostly over how to discipline JR. Things got so bad, they eventually divorced." She paused. "Do you really want to hear about this?"

Rafe did. "Yeah."

"Like you, JR also ended up moving in with Dad, who by then had retired from the army and moved to Seattle," she went on. "It was a bad decision, and as soon as JR turned eighteen, he dropped out of school and took off. No one in the family saw him for five years, although occasionally, he called to let Mom and me know he was okay. Then, in January, he showed up at my door with Chelsea, his pregnant, twenty-year-old girlfriend. Now she's about nine weeks along."

"That's awful young," Rafe said. "Although my mom was the same age when she had me."

"I'm happy JR found someone to love, but this isn't the best time for him and Chelsea to have a baby."

"I hear that. When my mom got pregnant, my dad was just a year older than JR and fresh out of law school."

"At least he had an education and a promising career ahead of him. My brother has nothing. No high school diploma or GED, and no way to take care of a family."

"Bummer. My mom used to call herself a hippie. Heck, she still does. She's been with a lot of guys, but she's never married. Not even when she got pregnant with me and my dad proposed. She claims she doesn't want to be under any man's thumb."

"That's understandable."

The comment didn't surprise him. After all, Jillian was also a free spirit. Hell, he felt the same way about letting a woman run over him. "My mom's choices made things a lot harder than they needed to be. The way we lived... I had a rough time." Neglected and undisciplined, Rafe had been a real handful. "I picked fights every chance I got and was headed for God knows what kind of trouble. When I was ten and she got tired of having me around, my dad took me in. He gave me structure and order and taught me about self-discipline. Saved my life."

Fierce love and profound gratitude filled Rafe's chest. "Everything I am today, I owe to him."

"Living with him was a good choice for you." Jillian looked wistful. "I only wish things had turned out as well for JR."

"I lucked out, that's for sure. Back to you. Growing up, you were the perfect daughter, trying hard to keep the peace in your house." Rafe pictured Jillian as a little girl, with all that responsibility on her young shoulders, and shook his head.

"How did you know? In the end, no matter how hard I tried and how good I was, it was never enough to make my parents happy."

Having been there with his mom, Rafe understood. "Putting yourself in charge of other people's happiness never works."

She gave a sad smile. "I know that now. Anyway, by the time I started my senior year in high school, things were really tense. Dad threatened to leave, and I knew it was only a matter of time before he and Mom divorced. I couldn't stand living in that house anymore, and the day after I graduated, I moved out. JR was only twelve, and I hated leaving him behind, but for my own sanity, I had to get away."

She frowned at a purple paint stain on her thumb, as if she wanted to avoid the judgment in Rafe's eyes. "Fast forward two years, to about a year after my parents divorced. JR was fourteen and too much for Mom to handle. She shipped him off to dear old Dad. The only reason JR stayed there until he was eighteen was because if he'd left when he was a minor, our father would have gone after him, brought him back, and done God knew what to punish him. End of story."

"Where did your brother go?"

"He's never really said." Although they were alone in the house, she leaned in and lowered her voice. "He's my only sibling and I missed him a lot, but to tell you the truth, it was kind of nice having him gone. A lot more peaceful for everyone. My mother remarried and moved to LA, and she and my dad are on speaking terms again. All the same, I'm glad he came back."

"If he earns his GED, he'll find a better job."

"Which I've pointed out several times. I even found the website for him to sign up for classes, but he isn't interested."

What could Rafe say to that? "Why are you letting him live with you?"

Her eyes widened. "I can't turn him and Chelsea out on the streets."

"Sure you can. It's called tough love. My dad laid down conditions and consequences if I didn't follow through. That worked with me."

"Well, my father's version failed miserably. And, don't forget, Chelsea's pregnant."

There was that. "You aren't your dad. You could try out the conditions and consequences idea on JR."

"I supposed so, but it's not my thing." Jillian glanced at the clock above the stove and jumped up. "Look at the time. If I want to finish painting before dark, I'd better get back to work."

To Rafe's astonishment, they'd talked nearly an hour. He didn't mind—he'd learned a lot about Jillian Metzger. Including that she was every bit the free spirit he'd imagined.

Still, what a knockout. Big, smoky-blue eyes and that great mouth... He thought about kissing her, to see if she tasted as good as she looked.

But the way they approached life was too different. And as Hank had pointed out, there was no sense getting involved with his neighbor when things would just turn sour later.

BY THE TIME Jillian finished the trim, the sun had tipped toward the horizon, and the temperature dropped into the shiver zone. After setting down her brush, she admired the building, which looked bright and cheerful and even better than she'd imagined. She squinted up at Rafe. "It's getting late. Time to quit."

"As soon as I finish the last little patch, up top." He strained toward the very peak of the building, his arm muscles flexing and his T-shirt hugging his strong back.

Jillian sucked in an admiring breath. As she'd worked on the trim, she'd thought a lot about their earlier conversation. Unlike most men, Rafe excelled at listening. She really liked that. Liked him. Even if he was a so-called stud.

She owed him for giving up his entire afternoon to help her. "You and Calvin should stay for dinner," she said. She'd been going to open a can of soup for herself, but Rafe needed heartier food. "I'm thinking about a pizza from Harvey's, and a nice can of dog food for Calvin."

"Pizza from the best place in town and food for my dog? That's a tough offer to turn down."

"Then, don't. You worked so hard, and feeding you is the least I can do. What are your favorite toppings?"

"Anything but pineapple."

"I happen to love pineapple. How about a compromise—half with, half without?"

"Deal."

Forty minutes and two bottles of beer later, Jillian set the extra-large pizza between them on the kitchen table. "Help yourself."

Rafe licked his lips and did just that. For a few minutes, they both concentrated on eating.

Before long, he slowed down and sat back. "How did you get into pottery?"

People rarely asked, but he seemed genuinely interested. "My sophomore year of high school, I needed an elective," she said. "My father pressured me to sign up for advanced math." She couldn't help making a face. "But the art teacher, Miss Patterson, suggested I enroll in her class. That sounded a lot more fun, so I fudged the truth and told Dad I needed a credit in art."

"He never checked your story?"

"Why would he? I was Miss Obedient—I would never make something up. That was my one tiny, rebellious act." Jillian smirked. "Besides, his fighting with my mother kept him too busy to look into the matter."

At the time, Jillian had been ripped apart by the strife at home and was lonely and miserable. The observant art teacher had taken her under her wing and made her feel valued and talented. "Miss Patterson mentored me. Under her wing, I blossomed. She taught me the basics of drawing and painting, but I liked throwing pots best. I loved taking a blob of clay and making it into something beautiful. Pottery became my passion. It still is."

"Passion is always a good thing."

Rafe's eyes darkened with unmasked desire. Jillian's most private places noticed. Self-conscious, she brushed crumbs from the tabletop into her palm.

After a minute, he cleared his throat. "What do you do when you're not making pottery, teaching pottery classes, or painting your studio?"

"You mean in my free time?" She laughed. "I rarely have any."

"Everyone needs a life outside of work."

"I wasn't raised that way."

"Come on. All work, no play..."

"Well..." She had to stretch to think of something. "I enjoy going to the movies. Sometimes I get together with friends for coffee or a meal. I date."

"Anyone special?" Rafe asked, his gaze hooded and unreadable.

She considered telling him how she wanted to find her Mr. Right, but she didn't know him well enough. "Not at the moment. What about you?" she asked. "What do you do when you aren't fighting fires or out running with friends?"

"I own rental property and do most of the repairs myself. That keeps me busy. And I buy old houses and renovate them to sell. This year, though, my main focus will be on the home I'm building."

"Are you planning to do the construction?"

He shook his head. "I want the house finished by fall. There's a lot to do, and I don't have time to tackle that job. I've already hired a construction company."

The whole idea put Jillian in awe. "That's so cool. I can't even imagine."

"I've been wanting to do this for a while, but I needed to find the right place. Now that I have, the house can't be built soon enough. Once I move in, I'll never move again."

"Ever?"

He shook his head. "During the first nine years of my life, my mother and I moved constantly. We never stayed anywhere for more than a few months."

"And I thought being an army brat meant moving a lot. I hated that, but I got used to it. So much so, that once I settled permanently in Guff's Lake, I kept moving around. But now that I've found this place with its perfect studio, I'll probably stay for a good long while. What about your dad? Did he move around, too?"

Rafe shook his head. "He's still in Sacramento, in the same house where he raised me. I want to put down roots, too."

"How do you know you won't get antsy and want something different?"

"I just know. It's all in here." He pointed to his head.

Jillian wished she was that certain about anything. "Half the time, I don't know what I'll want in an hour—except to make pottery."

"That's—"

The door suddenly opened, and Rafe never finished. JR and Chelsea burst in.

5

"I smell pizza," the tall kid who had to be JR said as he plodded into the kitchen. He and Jillian shared the same long limbs. His girlfriend followed, a skinny little thing except for the slightly rounded belly. JR eyed Rafe. "Who are you?"

Jillian frowned. "Don't be rude, JR."

Determined to make nice, Rafe stood and extended his arm. "Rafe Donato." He shook hands with Jillian's brother and nodded at the girl. "You're obviously JR and Chelsea."

Chelsea's eyebrows disappeared under cherry-red bangs before she smiled at Jillian.

JR gave Rafe a hard stare. "You're the guy who walked my sister home yesterday."

Rafe understood his wariness as a protective gesture toward his sister, and respected JR for it. "That's right."

The couple sat down, and JR started to reach for a slice of pizza.

"Hang on. I don't think your sister expected you

for dinner. She may have other plans for the rest of this pie," Rafe said.

"It's okay," she muttered, with obvious reluctance.

Again, JR reached for the pizza, and again, Rafe stopped him. "You might want to wash up before touching our food, man."

JR bristled. "Who the hell do you think you are?"

"I know exactly who I am—a senior firefighter who spent the afternoon helping your sister paint the outside of her studio because you didn't. And, yeah, I scrubbed up before dinner."

Rafe fixed JR with a straight-on look the younger man couldn't hold. His gaze dropped. Grumbling like a teenage kid, he pushed to his feet. Chelsea did the same, and they meandered down the hall, toward the bathroom.

"I'm in shock he actually obeyed you," Jillian commented.

"A guy can't argue washing his hands before he eats. They probably want to sit together."

Rafe scooted over, closer to Jillian. Under the small table, their thighs almost touched. She smelled good, of the great outdoors and beer and something sweet underneath that he definitely wanted to check out.

After returning from the bathroom, JR and his lady friend sat down and helped themselves.

"So, JR, I hear you're looking for a job," Rafe said while the two of them inhaled the remains of the pizza.

"That's right. I've applied for a couple things, but, so far, nothing has come through."

"What type of work are you looking for?"

"Anything."

"Tell me about your work experience."

"What is this, a job interview?"

Jillian sucked in an audible breath and stiffened. Her brother seemed to have an attitude problem. Rafe shrugged. "Just asking."

"I delivered fast food. I worked on a farm, clearing land to make a pasture and doing odd jobs. For a couple months, I apprenticed with a carpenter."

"What happened with that?"

"The boss was a mother fu— A butt."

It seemed clear JR was no picnic, either. "I'll keep my eyes and ears open for you," Rafe said.

"Thanks, man." JR shut the empty pizza box and nodded at Chelsea. "Let's go watch TV."

"How about cleaning up your mess first," Jillian said, sounding irritated.

"Chill, Jill. Okay."

After clearing their plates, the couple sauntered to the living room.

"You see what I'm dealing with," she said, compressing her pretty mouth into a thin line. "JR makes me want to scream! But Chelsea's sweet, even if she is too passive. And she is carrying my niece or nephew." A smile danced across her face.

"You're excited about that."

"You'd better believe it."

"What was that knowing look she gave you?"

"You saw that?" Jillian blushed. "She, um... She recognizes you from the calendar."

Rafe rolled his eyes.

"You don't like having your photo on it, huh?"

Rafe shook his head. "I do it because we bring a lot of money in to help others." Darkness had fallen, and he checked his watch. "I should get home."

He whistled for Calvin, stretched out on the kitchen floor. When the dog trotted to his side, he leashed him and stepped out the kitchen door and moored the leash to the stoop railing.

Jillian joined him. "Thanks again for your help."

In the cold air, her breath looked like wisps of smoke. Rafe nodded. "No problem."

Under the yellow porch light, he leaned down and brushed his lips over hers, a quick good night. But she tasted sweeter than he'd imagined, and one brief kiss wasn't enough. What started out as a casual gesture quickly flared into something bigger and hotter.

She responded immediately, wrapping her arms around his neck and kissing him back. Forgetting their philosophies on life were as different as night and day, Rafe angled closer, coaxed her lips apart, and deepened the kiss. He couldn't get enough. He even enjoyed the vague taste of pineapple.

In no time, he was ready to combust. He wanted to shed his clothes, strip hers away, and take her, right there against the siding.

The inferno raging through him brought him up short. This kind of thing didn't happen to him, not after a couple of kisses.

Confused and a little freaked, he tore his mouth away.

Jillian's eyelids fluttered open. She looked as dazed as he felt. Through sheer strength of will, he resisted pulling her in for more.

He unfastened Calvin from the railing and then offered a gruff, "Good night, Jillian."

"Night, Rafe."

He strode for his car.

THANKS TO A HABIT ramrodded into her by her father, Jillian had never been able to sleep in. Even after working into the wee hours Saturday night, she woke before dawn on Sunday, with a craving for a Samantha's cinnamon roll. She could get one at Rosemary's Breakfast Nook.

After showering and dressing, she scribbled a note for JR and Chelsea. This morning they deserved to sleep. For once, they'd pitched in, staying up late to install shelving for the six students who'd signed up for the four-week pottery class. Jillian reserved the two walls of existing shelves for her own work.

If the class went as well as she hoped, she would offer a more advanced version to the same group. She would also encourage them to post comments about the class on her website and to tell their friends about the class. In these ways, Jillian hoped to spread the word.

She let Pooh out and penned her in the fenced area. Only a week until the official first day of spring, and this morning the whole world seemed poised and ready. The air, crisp but not cold, the rising sun filling the sky with color, and the trill of songbirds in the newly leafed trees. Jillian couldn't help but be happy.

Humming the tune to "Sunshine Day," even though she couldn't carry a tune for anything, she climbed into her car and drove off. Normally, the trip from the cottage to Rosemary's took a good twenty minutes, but at this hour on a Sunday morning, she had the road to herself and made great time.

A few blocks from Rosemary's, she made an inexplicable detour, turning right instead of continuing straight. Seconds later, she passed the fire station. Rafe worked Mondays and Tuesdays, so, of course, he wasn't there today. All the same, she let out a soft sigh.

The man sure knew his way around a goodnight. It had been more than a week since he'd kissed her, but even thinking about it made her lips tingle and her whole body warm.

Absently, she touched her mouth and knew she wouldn't forget those amazing kisses anytime soon.

"Rafe Donato is trouble, plain and simple," she told herself out loud.

Although he wasn't nearly as rigid as she'd first assumed. Not at all like her father. Still, he apparently had a reputation even among his coworkers.

She didn't want to get involved with him, not when she hoped to meet her Mr. Right, settle down, and start a family. The sooner she stopped thinking about him, the better.

Resolved, she pulled into the mini-mall that housed Rosemary's Breakfast Nook.

Judging by the dozen or so parked cars grouped around the restaurant, she wasn't the only one out before eight a.m. on a Sunday. But then, Rosemary's served the best breakfast in town and was packed daily, from the second the doors opened at six a.m. until it closed at one.

The second Jillian entered the bustling restaurant, two things happened simultaneously. The delicious smells made her weak with hunger. She also spotted Rafe.

And just when she'd pushed him firmly from her mind. Why couldn't he have stayed home?

He and another man almost as handsome shared in a booth with an attractive female about Jillian's age, and a small boy seated next to Rafe. The boy chattered away at Rafe, and the firefighter's dimples winked charmingly.

Maybe that was why Jillian suddenly felt weak.

The angel sitting on her shoulder warned her to turn around and make a hasty exit, but the devil on her other shoulder prodded her to stay.

She was torn and hesitating when Rafe looked straight at her. For one long moment, their gazes locked. Jillian couldn't glance away.

She hadn't planned to approach the booth, and yet, suddenly, there she was. "Um, hi," she said, awkwardly fingering the strap of her purse. "I'm here to pick up some Samantha's cinnamon rolls."

Rafe nodded at the short, black-haired woman in the booth. "Meet Samantha Everett, the woman behind those treats."

"Wow," Jillian gushed. "I love all your stuff."

Samantha beamed. "That makes me happy." She elbowed the man beside her. "This big guy is Adam Healey. He and Rafe work together. The boy next to Rafe is my son, William."

"I recognize you from the firefighters calendar," Jillian told Adam. "You're Mr. January."

"One and the same." Like Rafe, he looked pained, as if the notoriety embarrassed him.

"Hey, it's a good thing," Samantha said. "That calendar raised a big chunk of money for the benefit fund. They're already talking about doing another next year."

"I'll definitely get one," Jillian said, exchanging smiles with Samantha.

"Me, too," William said. "When I grow up, I'm gonna be a firefighter just like Adam and Rafe."

Jillian smiled at the adorable boy. "That's great."

In the beat of silence that followed, her empty stomach rumbled. Embarrassed, she placed her hand over it.

"We haven't ordered yet," Samantha said. "Why don't you join us?"

Not wanting to intrude, Jillian shook her head. "I wouldn't want to impose."

"It's no big deal. We spend a lot of time together," Adam said. "Tell her, Rafe."

"A lot. Sit down." He nudged William over and then scooted across his side of the booth to make room for her.

There it was again—that intent, interested look. Jillian's heart fluttered and she went soft inside. But what was the point of eating with him and getting all worked up and even more attracted, when nothing would come if it? Nothing that would lead to what she really wanted—love and a baby.

She decided against sitting down.

"I really need to get back to the house," she said. "My first class is tomorrow night, and I still have tons to do."

"Class?" Samantha asked, raising her eyebrows a fraction.

"She makes pottery and she also teaches the craft," Rafe said.

Jillian nodded. "This will be my first class in my studio."

"I wish I had time to try my hand at pottery," Samantha said. "But with business booming... I'm getting ready to move into a commercial kitchen and hire my first assistant. Someday, though... Do you have a card?"

"I do. I also have a flyer." Jillian fished through her purse and handed over both. "My work is in several stores in the area. If you check my website, you'll find links to the stores and photos of some of my pieces. Or you can come to the Rogue Valley Arts Festival in Medford next month. I'll have a booth there. It was nice meeting you all. Enjoy your breakfast."

"I'll walk you out," Rafe said. "Adam, order me the usual."

"Coffee, the Rogue Valley omelet with hash browns, a side of bacon, and a warm cinnamon roll. Got it."

"You don't have to walk me out," Jillian said. "I

haven't even bought my cinnamon rolls yet, and there's a line."

"I'll wait with you. We should talk."

As they took their places behind some half-dozen customers, Jillian gave him a sideways look. "What are we supposed to talk about?"

"Tell you when we get outside."

She wondered what he wanted to say. If it was about those kisses on the back porch, he had nothing to worry about. She wasn't about to chase after him or expect anything.

An attractive female behind the counter placed three cinnamon rolls into a Rosemary's Breakfast Nook sack. She handed them to Jillian and gave Rafe a flirty smile. "How you doing today, Rafe?"

His dimples flashed. "Hey, Jana. Not bad. You got a new 'do. Nice."

"Thanks." Jana tossed her head, making her chin-length hair sway seductively. "I got it cut yesterday."

A jealous pang had Jillian frowning. Which was ridiculous, as well as confusing. She had no claim on Rafe and certainly didn't want one.

So why did she feel like clawing the waitress's eyes out?

6

Outside, eager to be alone with Jillian, Rafe shepherded her around the building toward the delivery area at the rear of the restaurant. At this hour on a Sunday, it stood empty.

"Hey," she said, digging in her heels. "My car is the other direction."

"And I'll get you there in a little while."

"You're not making sense." Jillian frowned. "I thought you wanted to talk about something—"

"I'm not interested in talking just now," he growled. Then he kissed her.

After a stunned intake of breath and a brief hesitation, she let go of the bakery sack, letting it drop to the ground. She twined her arms his neck and kissed him back.

When Rafe finally released her, she blinked a couple of times. "Why did you do that?"

"I wanted to see if you taste as good as I remembered." For good measure, he kissed her again. "You do."

With her eyes unfocused, her skin flushed, and her lips open a fraction, she looked thoroughly aroused. Sweet jeezus, she was sexy. He was going in for more when she pushed hard against his chest with her palms.

"Stop it, Rafe." Her gaze had become razor-sharp, and displeasure turned her lush mouth down at the corners.

Clueless as to what had just happened, he eyed her. "What'd I do?"

"I don't hear from you for over a week, not even a text. Then I accidentally run into you. You say you want to talk, but instead you drag me out back and kiss me? I don't think so."

Her enthusiastic response belied her words, but he wasn't fool enough to point that out. "I haven't been in touch because I've been trying to stay away from you," he explained.

That was true. He wanted her in a way he hadn't wanted a woman in a long time. Ever. That scared him.

"Then why did you kiss me?"

"Because when I'm around you, it's all I think about." And also when he wasn't with her. This past week, he'd thought of little else.

Her exhale was pure scorn. "If you were the tiniest bit interested in me, you'd call or email or text. You'd ask me out."

While he worked out how to respond, she dropped a zinger. "I wouldn't go out with you anyway. I'm not interested."

He wasn't used to hearing that. "You kiss like

you are." He ran his thumb over her lower lip. Her pupils dilated, and her mouth relaxed into fullness. Satisfied, he grinned. "You want me, all right."

She batted his hand away. "That has nothing to do with it."

She'd totally lost him. He gave her a sideways look. "I don't understand."

"It's simple. I want to have a baby."

Say what? Rafe stepped back. "Not with me, you don't. I like you, and I'm attracted as hell to you, but I'm not nearly ready to be a dad. I'm not sure I ever will be."

Her eyes sparked with anger. "Of all the cocky... I don't want to have a baby with *you*. We don't know each other well enough to even consider it. I just thought you should know I'm looking for a man who's ready to settle down, get married, and start a family."

The statement stunned him. "The other day, when I mentioned my mom and how she never married because she didn't want to be under any man's thumb, you said you understood."

"I do, but I don't necessarily agree with her."

He put both hands up, palms out, and stepped back. "I'm not the marrying kind."

"I know. You're a stud."

"The guys only call me that because they know it bugs me."

"All I know is, what you want and what I want are two different things. That rules you out for me."

"You got that right." Rafe couldn't get away from Jillian and her need to get married and procreate fast enough. "You dropped your cinnamon rolls." He scooped her bakery bag from the pavement and handed it to her.

He didn't draw a normal breath until they turned in opposite directions and went their separate ways.

AS THE FIRST pottery class wound down Monday evening, Jillian mentally swiped her brow. So far, so good.

The six pottery novices sitting at the studio worktable, all female, ranged in age from about thirty to sixty-something. Tonight's session had been devoted to the basics—working with clay and getting familiar with the potter's wheel—and they seemed to be enjoying themselves.

With less than thirty minutes remaining, it was time to field any final questions.

Patty, a self-described middle-aged housewife with empty nest syndrome, raised her hand. "I'm worried my clay will dry out before class next week. How do I keep that from happening?"

"It can easily dry out, so I'm glad you asked." Jillian demonstrated how to wrap the clay in wet paper towels and seal it in a plastic bag. "Go ahead and do that now. There are paper towels in the dispenser next to the sink at the back of the studio."

She waited for everyone to comply before she nodded at the shelves JR and Chelsea had installed. "The empty shelf space is for you to store your clay and whatever you make during class. Be sure to label your space so you don't accidentally take someone else's clay. Next week, you'll be throwing the pots we'll eventually fire in the kiln."

Excited murmurs filled the studio.

"I hope mine looks half as pretty as yours," Edie, a grandmotherly woman, commented.

Jillian had shown her students her own work-in-progress drying on the shelves, along with photos of the pieces she'd sold through the years. "I wouldn't worry too much about that," she said. "It took me years to get where I am now. With time and practice, you'll get there, too. That reminds me. When these sessions end, I'm planning to teach a more advanced class. I'd love to see you come back. Are there any last questions before you leave?"

Wanda, a hair stylist about Jillian's age, posed the next question. "Even though I wore an old smock, I got clay on my tights and under my nails. How do I get it out?"

"I use a nail scrub brush on my hands. For clothes, I let the clay dry and then brush the excess off. Any residue usually washes out."

A pretty redheaded woman named Nora spoke next. "This has nothing to do with pottery, but it is related to this class. Being divorced and on the market, I hoped to meet guys here. Why didn't any sign up?"

Jillian grinned. "When I taught at the Artist Cooperative school, I did have one or two men in my class who went on to become decent potters. I did hand out flyers to some of the firefighters from the

Guff's Lake Fire Department, but as you can see, none of them signed up."

Not that she'd expected anyone from the crew who worked with Rafe. Monday nights, they were all on duty.

Nora glanced at the calendar on the wall, and at the color photo hunky Mr. March, the same Gus whom Jillian had met the other day, and sighed. "Too bad. Maybe you can introduce me around?"

"I don't know the firefighters that well," she said.

Except maybe Rafe. But the thought of introducing him to Nora or any other woman didn't sit well with Jillian. Even if his negative reaction to the idea of marriage and kids made her all the more determined to steer clear of him.

But, oh, when he gave her that intent, steamy look... Ignoring the warmth flooding her, she ushered her students out. As soon as they drove away, she headed to the house to find JR, who had promised to help clean up after class.

She couldn't find him anywhere. She peeked in the spare bedroom he and Chelsea had taken over. Chelsea was alone and curled up under the covers. Lying on the floor next to her, Pooh raised her head and woofed softly. The girl stirred and offered a sleepy smile. "What time is it?"

"A little after ten."

"I was so tired, I climbed into bed early."

"No wonder. You're pregnant. You need your rest. Where's JR?"

Chelsea yawned. "He went out with a friend from high school."

Jillian hadn't realized he'd reconnected with any

of his old friends, guys he hadn't seen since before he'd moved to Seattle. "Which friend, and where did they go?"

"I think his name is Pete? They went out for a beer."

With what money? JR didn't have any to spare. Jillian remembered Pete as a partier and a trouble-maker. Of course, he could have changed since then. Still, she was uneasy. She frowned. "JR was supposed to help me clean up the studio after class tonight."

"I didn't realize. I can do it."

Not about to interrupt the rest of the mother-to-be of her niece or nephew, Jillian shook her head. "Never mind. Go on back to sleep."

Chelsea didn't argue. She lay back down. Jillian slipped out of the room and shut the door behind her.

While she scrubbed clay off the work-table and vacuumed, she muttered and worried about her brother. He'd better not fall in with the wrong crowd, not with a baby on the way.

She was fed up with his sneakiness and broken promises, and done letting him off the hook while she did everything and he goofed off. It was time he grew up, found work, and moved out. Which he apparently wasn't going to do without a push.

Tough love, Rafe had advised. Although she bristled at the very idea, she had to do something.

She would ask him to leave by a certain date. Nothing in the too-immediate future, but she would set a definite date. She would tell him in a gentle, loving voice, rather than using the harsh, rigid tones her father favored.

No matter how she said it, JR wouldn't like it. But he'd brought this on himself. The next time she saw him, she would tell him.

7

A t the Guff's Lake Fire Department, Rafe wore many hats, including teaching fire safety classes around town, conducting building inspections, and a host of other tasks. He divided most of his time between two main jobs—firefighter and paramedic. This was his month to serve as a paramedic. With two cardiac arrests, a concussion, and several additional medical calls, it had been a long day. Tonight could be equally busy or slow enough to grab some much-needed Zs.

Evenings, each firefighter took a turn cooking dinner for the whole crew, while someone else cleaned up. Having fulfilled his food duties the previous month, Rafe could do other things. Taking advantage of the momentary lull in activity after the massive spaghetti dinner Max had cooked and served up, Rafe descended the stairs to the apparatus bay, aka the garage. Near the aid car, he laid out a clean, pressed paramedic shirt, his paramedic windbreaker, and shoes. When the next call came, he could quickly climb into them.

He checked his watch and thought about Jillian. By now, her pottery class was in full swing. He wondered how that was going, caught himself, and frowned.

She wanted to get married and have a baby, and he wasn't going to think about her anymore, period.

Yet, here he was, doing exactly that.

Kissing her behind Rosemary's had done a real number on him. He shouldn't have done it, but there was something about her that drove him wild. Her long-limbed, slender body, for one. Slender, but not skinny, with curves that were all woman. And her mouth...

His body woke up, and he started to get hard.

Hell.

Setting his jaw, he strode into the garage, where several of the guys were prepping for future calls and doing other stuff.

Adam was finishing up with a call on his cell phone. "Love you, babe," he said, with the goofy smile he got when he talked to Sam.

They had a good thing going on, might even make it long term.

For both their and little William's sakes, Rafe hoped so. While he was happy for them, he didn't understand love and for sure didn't want it. Watching his mother ruin numerous relationships and reel in the aftermath, and witnessing his father's suffering when his marriage to Lori had soured had been awful. Rafe would never set himself up for that kind of pain.

"Up for a game of hearts?" he asked when Adam had finished his call and laid out his stuff.

They had an unwritten rule to not play poker at the station. That they reserved for Friday nights, with a standing game at a different coworker's house each week and everyone from the station welcome. Sometimes ten people showed, sometimes two or three. Lately, Rafe hadn't played at all.

"Okay." Adam nodded to Hank. "You in?"

"Sure. Hey, Liam, how about a game of hearts?"

Wearing the trademark scowl guaranteed to intimidate people who didn't know him, the giant of a man shrugged. "Sure, if you suckers don't mind getting your asses trounced."

With the usual blustering, the four of them climbed the stairs to the kitchen/dining area, which doubled as a place for group relaxation.

Rafe grabbed a worn deck of cards from the game shelf, and they sat down at one end of the big, rectangular dinner table. After shuffling, he dealt the cards.

"Seen Jillian lately?" Hank asked as he collected his hand.

"I've been hearing about her," Liam commented. "She lives on the property next to yours. She's supposed to be hot." A cocky grin transformed his whole face. "When do I get to meet her?"

Rafe narrowed his eyes, silently warning the dude to steer clear.

"Lighten up, Rafe." Liam rubbed his hand over his shaved head before throwing down the two of clubs.

Rafe tossed in a card.

"I met her last week, near the end of our run,"

Hank said. "She has legs you wouldn't believe."

"I saw her at Rosemary's yesterday, when Sam, William, Rafe, and I met for breakfast there," Adam said.

Liam raised his eyebrows. "She ate with you?"

Rafe frowned. "No, and quit looking at me that way. I don't plan to see her again."

"Why not?"

"For starters, she's not my type. Plus, getting involved with my future neighbor is a bad idea. And because she said point blank she's ready to get married and have a baby."

Liam looked stricken. Like Rafe, he enjoyed playing the field. He shrugged. "At least she's up front about what she wants."

Over the PA system, Sarah McCone, one of the female dispatchers who worked for the fire and police departments, called out a fire alarm at Barclay's Pub at the north end of town.

Leaving the cards on the table, Rafe and his buds quickly moved toward the brass fire pole, used only when a call came in. One by one, they slid down it and prepared to head out.

To Rafe's relief, the fire at Barclay's Pub caused only minor damage. He, Ethan, and Gus, this month's paramedic team, checked out all the customers. None showed any indications of smoke inhalation or medical trauma. Given the rapid response time of the fire department, that came as no surprise.

Unlike finding JR Metzger on the premises. He appeared to be sober, but his staggering sidekick, a skinny, scraggly looking male, was obviously drunk.

"How you doing?" Rafe asked JR.

"Not bad. I've never been at a tavern when a fire broke out. At first, it was kind of exciting."

"There's nothing exciting about a fire in a building full of people," Rafe countered. Although, truth be told, every time a call came into the department, adrenaline surged through the whole crew. "Be thankful our firefighters extinguished the fire quickly and no one got hurt."

"Good point."

"Why don't you call your sister and your girlfriend. They'll want to hear you're all right."

"They won't know about this fire. Besides, it's almost eleven o'clock. These days, Chelsea's never up past ten. Jillian's probably winding down and getting ready to turn in. I'll tell them in the morning." JR glanced at his friend. "Ready to take me home?"

"If I were you, I wouldn't ride with this guy," Rafe advised. He nodded at the other man. "You're in no shape to drive."

The intoxicated male bristled. "I'm fine."

Safety was key, and in the interest of calming him down, Rafe gentled his tone. "Come on, buddy, it's obvious you've had too much to drink."

"How the hell would you know, you son of a bit—"

JR grabbed his friend's arm. "He's right, Pete. You're drunk. Besides, the cops over there are watching us."

Muttering, Pete quickly backed down, pulled his cell phone from his pocket, and punched in a number.

"You do the same, JR," Rafe said.

The kid shifted his weight. "I, uh, don't have a cell phone."

Without a job he probably didn't have the funds to buy one. Rafe pulled his own phone from his pocket. "Here, borrow mine."

JR made the call and then returned Rafe's phone. "Jillian's going to pick me up."

Not exactly the woman Rafe wanted to see, but he figured he could handle himself by playing it cool.

Pete's ride showed up. Soon, only JR, the tavern owner, a police officer, Rafe, and his crewmates remained.

Rafe told Ethan and Gus to stand by while he talked to JR. His two crewmates began to pack up.

"What are you doing, hanging out with a guy like Pete?" he asked.

JR scrubbed his hand over his face. "We haven't really hung out since before I moved to Seattle in ninth grade. Pete's not so bad. He said he might know of a job for me at the bottling plant where he works. We were discussing it over beers."

Jillian's hatchback pulled into the parking lot. The rush that went through Rafe had nothing to do with the fire. "Your sister's here, in record time. Your call probably scared her."

"You're the one who asked me to call her." JR rolled his eyes. "Sometimes she acts more like a mom than a sister."

She exited her car, her long legs encased in leggings and boots that looked sexy on her. Her forehead wrinkled with concern, she hurried toward her brother. "Are you okay, JR?"

He gave a terse nod and brushed off the hug, reminding Rafe of a teenage kid who didn't want anyone fussing over him.

Ethan and Gus and the men from the two fire trucks wandered over. Rafe figured those who knew Jillian wanted to say hello. The others no doubt wanted introductions.

Within minutes, she'd greeted the men she already knew and had met the rest, along with Captain Comings.

Warm, friendly, and clearly comfortable in her own skin, she charmed them all, Rafe included. Even if he was bound and determined to play it cool. He might not want the white picket fence and all the trimmings, but he sure wanted her.

After a few minutes of chitchat, the firefighters disbursed. Rafe asked Ethan and Gus to hang loose a little longer, and the two moved toward the aid car.

"Did your pottery class go okay?" he asked Jillian, careful to hide his unwelcome warmth.

"Until the end." Her eyes narrowed at her brother. "I need speak with you for a minute. We'll be right back, Rafe."

Rafe nodded and used the time to organize his gear in the medical kit he'd brought. Although Jillian and her brother kept their voices low, he could hear snatches of the conversation.

"...agreed to help me clean up after class," she

said. "But no, you..."

Between her angry expression and tone, Rafe easily filled in the gaps. JR had chosen to hang with Pete instead of helping Jillian.

A mixture of guilt and defensiveness darkened JR's face. "It was a spur of the moment thing," he said, his voice carrying easily. "Pete said he might know of a job at the bottling plant."

"A job?" Her tone softened. "That'd be so great."

"Yeah, but according to Pete, they're looking for certified welders. That leaves me out." Hanging his head, JR kicked at a pebble.

"At least Pete knows you're looking. You did tell him to put out word you need work."

Her brother stiffened. "Come on, Jill, I'm not that dumb. Of course I did. I don't need you telling me how to look for a job."

Jillian crossed her arms and raised her voice. "Seeing as you haven't lined up a single interview, apparently, you do."

"Get off my back!"

Every person within hearing distance stared at them.

She winced, and Rafe's protective hackles rose. Forget that he meant to play it cool. He moved closer to Jillian, but she signaled for him to leave them alone. He nodded, but hovered nearby.

"I hate that you're upset with me," she told her brother. "As much as I love you, I'm not thrilled with you, either. You haven't followed through on your promise to give me a hand when I need you, and I don't see you spending much time looking for a job. I'll help in any way I can, but this can't go on forever. You have three months, until mid-June, to find work, save up, and move into your own place. Then you have to go."

She'd used a form of tough love that impressed Rafe. Maybe she'd given her brother more time to get his act together than Rafe would have, but at least she'd set an end date. And she'd done it with love and loyalty to JR that had shone through.

Rafe couldn't help but compare her to his mother, a woman without a loyal bone in her body or a thought for anyone but herself. Some of his earliest memories were of when she left him alone in the evening, sometimes for the entire night, and then lied about where she'd stayed and with whom.

Jillian was straight-forward and steady. And he hated what her brother put her through.

With that, he made a snap decision. He crossed to where they stood and joined them. "I couldn't help overhearing. I might be able to help," he told JR. "You've cleared pastureland, so I assume you can operate a chainsaw and drive a bulldozer." He waited for JR's nod then continued. "Before the builder can break ground on my house, I need to clear half an acre of brush and small to medium-size trees. It's a two-person job and should take ten days to two weeks to finish. You interested?"

JR brightened right up. "Hell, yes."

Jillian's brilliant smile made Rafe feel ten feet tall.

"All right, then," he said. "I go off duty at zero eight hundred Wednesday morning. Why don't we meet at my property after lunch, and I'll show you what I want. The following week, you can start."

"Awesome. Do I need to find a partner to work with?"

"That's taken care of." Rafe had already contracted with a tree removal expert he trusted, a man who wouldn't be averse to taking on JR instead of his own assistant—provided Rafe paid extra. He wasn't about to analyze why he wanted to do this. "His name is Zach, and you'll meet him Wednesday."

"What about the equipment? Should rent my own tools?"

Rafe shook his head. "Zach has everything."

Knowing he'd pleased Jillian made him way too happy. As he ambled toward the aid car, he caught himself grinning and quickly sobered. No sense giving his buddies any ideas when he planned to steer clear of her.

He climbed into the back of the aid car and buckled in.

"If I stood in your shoes, I'd be grinning, too," Gus quipped from the passenger seat. "She's a looker, all right. Chalk up another score for our resident stud."

So much for wiping his expression clean. "You're one to talk," Rafe returned. At six feet four, two hundred thirty pounds of solid muscle and an outgoing personality, Gus had no problem attracting women.

"Jillian didn't give me that soft-eyed smile."

"In case you haven't heard, she's on the prowl for a husband."

"Ah." Gus shook his head. "That changes everything."

8

---

elighted with the luscious blue-green glaze and the shimmering gold edging she'd applied to a recently fired sushi set, Jillian whistled. "You are gorgeous, if I do say so."

Once she fired the pieces for the second time, a process permanently fixing the glaze, the colors would be even more vivid. The tray and bowls could then be used for sushi or appetizers, or simply appreciated as art.

Jillian intended to sell it and a bunch of other pottery at the next month's art festival. She would also bring scrapbooks of other work and take custom orders to fill later.

If all went as planned, she would net a hefty chunk of change. Money she needed. Mainly because, between the loss of income due to the closure of the school at the Artist Cooperative and the larger than usual grocery bills, courtesy of JR and Chelsea, her bank balance had dropped too low for comfort.

She carefully arranged the sushi pieces on a

shelf to dry undisturbed, where they joined dozens of other recently glazed items. All of it ready for the kiln.

At the sink, Jillian washed up, humming loud enough to hear herself over the hiss of the water. Then she laughed at herself for sounding so off-key.

The pretty pottery contributed to her good mood. That and JR's job. At this very minute, her brother was with Rafe, learning about his upcoming job. And icing on the cake—JR had accepted her timeline to move out. Rafe had been right. When done well, tough love wasn't such a bad thing.

If that wasn't wonderful enough, this very minute Chelsea had gone out to apply for a sales job at the Rogue Valley Cheesery, a shop that sold handmade cheese near the Guff's Lake resort. This was the first job she'd applied for since she and JR had shown up. It seemed his temporary employment had jump-started her to look for work.

Wouldn't it be great if they both got jobs? They could save up quickly for a place of their own and be out before mid-June.

Mentally, Jillian crossed her fingers, but she knew she was getting ahead of herself. In order to pay rent on his own apartment, JR needed a permanent, full-time job and a paycheck he could depend on. Finding that would probably take the full three-month deadline she'd given them.

Baby steps first. For now, she was grateful Rafe had given her brother a chance to prove himself.

He didn't have to do that. What a great guy. She liked him more all the time.

If only he wanted to settle down and start a family...

"Knock-knock," Chelsea said, entering the studio.

"Hey." Jillian smiled. "How was the interview?"

"Oh, you know."

That didn't sound so good. "Not great, huh?"

"It wasn't terrible. I got along with the woman who interviewed me, and she liked my restaurant and retail experience. But I doubt she'll hire me."

"Why not?"

Chelsea gave her a duh look. "Because I'm pregnant." She laid a hand over her belly, which seemed to grow by the day.

"She wouldn't dare. It's illegal to discriminate."

"She'd never admit the reason."

"All the same, I'm going to think positive and keep my fingers crossed," Jillian said.

Chelsea shrugged. "I wish I could call JR. When will he be back?"

Yet another thing the couple desperately needed—cell phones. "We'll see him when we see him."

"I can't wait for him to have money." The girl hugged herself and spun around.

It was pretty exciting. Even temporary work had boosted his self-confidence. He wasn't as ready to take offense at things Jillian said, and had even cracked a joke or two. His brighter attitude was bound to translate into good things, such as putting more effort into searching for a permanent job. And then... Jillian stopped herself right there. There she went, getting ahead of herself again.

"Are you ready for a coffee break?" Chelsea asked. "Except you don't drink coffee, and my doctor won't let me."

Pleased that Chelsea wanted her company, Jillian smiled. "Your timing is perfect. I just finished for the day. Who needs coffee when there's tea for me and cocoa mix for you?"

As they exited the studio into the weak afternoon sun, Pooh barked excitedly. They collected her from the fenced area and brought her with them.

While water for the tea heated and Chelsea stirred cocoa into a steaming mug of milk, Jillian opened a package of chocolate cookies and set it on the table. Pooh sat down nearby with her ears cocked and her tail wagging hopefully. "Sorry, girl, these will make you sick."

Chelsea grinned. "I got that covered," she said, shoving a couple of doggie treats into her jeans pocket.

Soon they were seated at the table, sipping their drinks and munching on cookies.

From time to time, Chelsea fed Pooh a treat. "At the interview, I heard about the big ash tree near Guff's Lake," she said. "Do you believe what they say?"

Local folklore surrounded the centuries-old tree, which stood some six yards from Guff's Lake. Supposedly, if a couple kissed under the tree, theirs would be a lasting love.

Jillian had never been kissed under the tree, not even by Douglas. "Actually, I do."

Chelsea was silent for a moment, and Jillian guessed she wanted JR to take her to the tree.

After hemming and hawing, the girl bit her lip. "Can I ask you something, Jillian?"

"If it's about my brother, I have no idea what he'll do."

"Huh?" Chelsea said, with a blank look. "This is about work. If I don't get the job at the Rogue Valley Cheesery... Do you think you could hire me as your assistant?"

She'd never shown any interest in making pottery, but, then, Jillian hadn't exactly encouraged her. "I'm flattered, and I think you'd make a great assistant. The problem is, I'm barely making enough money to cover my own expenses, let alone pay you. Although you never know. If my classes take off... Maybe. First you'd need to learn pottery basics."

"But I need a job right away." Chelsea's shoulders slumped. "I understand. I'll keep looking."

She didn't seem interested in learning about pottery. Still, she did have retail sales experience... Jillian had an idea. "The Rogue Valley Arts Festival I've been working so hard to get ready for is a little more than three weeks away. I expect to be busy day and night, and I'd appreciate an extra pair of hands. Maybe you can help me out then?"

Chelsea's somber expression lifted. "You mean it? Thanks, Jill."

"The festival only lasts three days, with an extra day needed to set up the booth and a long night taking it apart again Sunday evening. I won't be able to pay you much."

"Anything is better than zero."

Suddenly, Pooh's ears pricked up. With a joyous woof, she scrambled up and raced for the door. Jillian recognized the sound of the purring engine. Her heart bumped hard in her chest. "Isn't that Rafe's car? He must be bringing JR home."

Chelsea stood. "I thought he would walk back."

Jillian half hoped Rafe would drop off JR and leave. Given her growing feelings for him, that would be the safest route.

She let Chelsea go out alone and waited a few minutes, listening for the revving engine to tell her when Rafe drove away. But all she heard were Calvin's woof and Pooh's responding yip. Curious and unable to help herself, she slipped out the door.

Rafe had exited the car. Calvin wagged his tail at Pooh, who pranced with excitement. Despite the cool afternoon temperature, Rafe wore no jacket. In a navy T-shirt and jeans, he looked so good she wanted to drool. He sauntered toward her, while JR moved toward Chelsea with a swagger in his step.

He put his arm around Chelsea and grinned. "Zach and I start a week from today."

They shared a quick kiss, followed by a meaningful look. Arms around each other, they headed into the house, leaving Pooh behind to frolic with Calvin. And Jillian alone with Rafe and the dogs.

She wanted the same things—a kiss, a meaningful look, and the promise of a lot more. Just now, her feelings for Rafe were so strong, she tucked her hands under her arms to keep from reaching for him.

"So it went okay?" she asked, impressed she sounded totally normal.

He nodded. "Even with Zach's expertise and the two of them working, the job won't be easy. But I think JR will manage."

Jillian crossed her fingers—and decided to share her doubts. "My brother doesn't have the best track record for sticking with things," she warned. "Especially when the task is difficult."

"I'm not worried."

She released the breath she'd been holding. "Thanks for giving him this opportunity, Rafe. I... we all...appreciate this."

"My pleasure."

Pleasure. The word whispered across her suddenly feverish skin. Rafe's eyes had gone as warm and as dark as melted chocolate. Jillian felt the heat radiating from him. A wave of longing rushed through her. She stepped back, away from his magnetic pull, but the heat stayed with her.

"Chelsea applied for a job at the Rogue Valley Cheesery," she said, pretending to be unaffected. "She also asked to be my assistant."

"Are you going to hire her?"

"I can't afford to. Besides, she isn't really interested in making pottery. But I did hire her to work in my booth at the art festival."

Rafe nodded. "I see you've been working today."

The corner of his mouth lifted, and she groaned. "Let me guess. I have clay on my face again."

"Right there." He pointed at her cheek.

Good thing he didn't touch her. Otherwise, she

just might go up in flames. She wet her finger and then rubbed at the spot. "Gone?"

"Yeah." Rafe had been watching closely, his expression impossible to read. "I've never been in a pottery studio before. Do you have time to show it to me?"

Jillian had no idea why he looked taken aback by his own question. He certainly surprised her. Aside from students and fellow potters, few guys had ever asked.

"You really want to see my studio?" she asked, pathetically excited to give him a tour. But also a little nervous. She really needed to get away from him and cool off. "I don't allow pets in there. Animal hair tends to muck up my glazes."

"As long as Calvin can hang out in the fenced area with Pooh, he'll be fine."

She would keep the tour short and professional, she assured herself while she and Rafe penned in the dogs. Then she'd send Rafe on his way. That should be harmless enough.

"Follow me." She beckoned him to join her.

9

What was he doing, heading into Jillian's studio? Rafe silently chided himself. Sure, he wanted to see her work space, but with his desire for her barely in check, this probably wasn't a smart idea.

She shut the door behind them and gestured around. "This is where all the magic happens."

The studio was bigger it looked from the outside, spacious even. Yet, at the same time, surprisingly cozy. Despite blinds pulled against the afternoon sun, a skylight overhead provided plenty of natural light over the clean concrete floor, the big, scarred table, and the faded sofa well past its prime. A pottery wheel sat off to one side, not far from a wall of cabinets and two open shelves filled with pottery.

Rafe nodded at the Guff's Lake Fire Department calendar hanging near a bulletin board, and the photo of Gus grinning. "Good to see you actually use that thing."

For the first time since he'd brought JR home, she cracked a smile. "Hey, I consider it my civic duty to support your benefit fund. You can see why I renewed my lease on the cottage."

"This is some studio." He noted the bulging shelves. "You sure have a lot of pottery over there."

"Most of it is for the upcoming art festival. There are lots more, packed and waiting, in the cabinets. Those you see need to be kiln-fired a second time. As soon as I have room, I'll create more."

"How many pieces are you planning to make?"

"According to my inventory spreadsheet, I need at least double what I have."

Rafe had never figured her for the spreadsheet type. "You keep a tally of your inventory?"

She nodded. "I also track orders and sales. If I want to stay on top of my business, I have to."

He'd had no idea she was so organized and practical, or that she worked this hard. She wasn't nearly as flaky as he'd thought.

On another wall, blocks of clay wrapped in plastic bags sat on a smaller group of shelves. "What's all that?"

"My students' supplies. This week, they learned the basics of working with clay. Next Monday, they throw their first pots."

"That should be interesting."

"And messy, and frustrating for some. Crafting a piece of pottery is harder than it looks. My plan is to have fun and hope everyone signs up for more advanced classes. Of course, I'll also ask them to post comments on my website and spread the word to their friends and acquaintances."

"Cool idea to use your website that way." Rafe wandered over to the shelves of Jillian's pieces and whistled. "Some of this is amazing."

She flushed with pleasure. "Thanks. So JR's job will last between ten days and two weeks?"

"Probably. If things work out and Zach is satisfied with your brother's work, he may decide to keep him on," he said, wanting to keep the pleased look on her face. "But that's up to Zach. Don't say anything to JR."

"I won't." She rewarded him with a brilliant smile, so beautiful he couldn't look away. "Why are you doing this, Rafe?"

For her. He wasn't about to dig any further than that. "Because your brother needs work, and I need someone to clear my land."

"This means a lot to me. To us." She bit her lip, drawing his attention to her sexy mouth, and then stepped closer. "Thank you so much." Leaning in, she brushed his cheek with those lips.

Did she have any idea what that did to him? Not about to light a match to that particular fire, Rafe froze. Her hair smelled like spring, and, underneath, he caught a whiff of clay and sunshine and woman.

Revving up, straight into overdrive, growing harder by the second, he gritted his teeth. "What are you doing?"

"It's a thank-you kiss." Her flushed cheeks and darkened eyes belied the words.

Rafe meant to back away. Instead, he wrapped his arms around her. "I'm not the marrying kind," he warned, his vanishing hold on his self-control making his voice gruff.

"At the moment, I don't care."

"You should. I—"

"Stop talking and kiss me."

She wrapped her arms around his neck and tugged him down. And he was lost.

RAFE'S KISS was different than before. More demanding, almost ravenous, sparking Jillian's own hunger. When he skimmed his palms up her sides, she tensed with expectation. His thumbs brushed across her nipples, and the breath fluttered from her lips.

To her dismay, he stopped and tore his mouth from hers. "Do you want me to stop?"

She could barely think, let alone form words. After returning his hands to her aching breasts, she pulled him into another kiss.

Rafe seemed to sense when her knees were about to buckle. With his lips fused to hers, he backed her toward the sofa and drew her down. It was too short for them to stretch out fully, and Jillian ended up on his lap.

He lifted the hem of her long-sleeved T-shirt up over her bra, unfastened the front clasp, and pushed it aside. Cool air washed over her hot skin. She shivered.

His molten gaze slid over her. "You have beautiful breasts."

"I've always wished they were bigger."

"They're perfect, with the prettiest pink nipples." With his finger, he traced one areola. "Tight, like rosebuds."

Oh, the pleasure. Suddenly damp between her legs, Jillian let her head fell back and thrust out her chest, silently offering herself.

With a masculine growl of desire, Rafe lowered his head and pleasured her with his mouth.

Sheer bliss. Longing for more, she shifted restlessly in his lap.

"Easy," he cautioned, grasping her hips and holding her still.

Dazed, she blinked at him. The man looked as if he was in pain. "Did I hurt you?"

"Not exactly." His lips quirked. "This feels more like torture."

Hot hands skated down her stomach. The button on her jeans had always been slightly bigger than the buttonhole, and difficult to unfasten.

Would he have trouble with it? Jillian caught her breath. But no, he deftly worked it open, like the experienced man, the *stud*, he was.

Her guarded heart, open and tender, contracted in alarm, all but destroying her desperate need for him. "Don't, Rafe."

He went still. "Okay." In short order, he zipped up her jeans, tugged her shirt down, and set her on the cushion beside him. "Maybe we should talk."

~

RAFE DESIRED Jillian more than he could ever remember wanting a woman. And she was just as hot for him, which was a total turn-on. But she'd been right to stop him.

"As bad as I want you, Jillian, what we're doing is crazy," he said, for both her sake and his. "You're looking for marriage and kids, and we both know I'm the wrong man for that."

She nodded and blew out a heavy breath. "When we're apart, that's easy to remember. But when we're together and your eyes go hot and dark and focused... Then it's hard to recall what I want. While you were kissing me and touching me... I didn't want us to stop." Hesitating, she glanced down at her hands for a moment. "I never felt this way before, and it scares me."

Rafe appreciated her honesty, but the words made him plenty nervous. "I don't want to be the guy who breaks your heart."

Her eyes flashed. "You think I do? I'm not falling for you, Rafe. I just... I have this physical thing for you that won't let go."

"You're talking about sex." Relief washed over him. He glanced down at the hard-on about to bust his fly open. "As you can see, I'm on the same page. The chemistry between us is off the charts."

"Exactly. And it's keeping me from even looking at another man. I'm not at all sure how to fix that."

Through the closed studio windows, Rafe heard the dogs barking and JR's voice. Thank God for the shuttered blinds. He'd been so hot for Jillian, he hadn't even thought about privacy.

Hadn't thought, period. He shook his head in disbelief. But then, the same thing had happened the first time they'd kissed. With one big difference—today had been more intense.

His cell phone rang. He slid it from his hip pocket and glanced at the screen. "It's Adam. I'm supposed to be at his place, to help install a new shower. One of the many things he wants done before Sam and William move in this summer. Excuse me."

Jillian nodded and showed her back to him while she fastened her bra. Rafe also turned away, giving her privacy.

"Hey, Adam. I lost track of the time. I'll be over shortly." He disconnected.

When he faced her again, she'd smoothed her T-shirt into place and buttoned her jeans. She looked as if nothing had happened—if you didn't count her flushed skin and kiss-swollen lips.

Beautiful and passionate. Irresistible.

Unable to keep his hands off her, Rafe brushed her silky-soft hair from her face, his hungry fingers lingering on the delicate shells of her ears. Her eyes went soft again, and her lips parted, testing his willpower to the max.

He shoved his hands into his pockets. "Look, I don't want to mess with your plans to find a guy who shares your dreams for the future. We probably shouldn't see each other anymore, especially not alone. I'm not saying we should go out of our way to avoid each other, but if we are together, we'd best make sure other people are around."

"Agreed." Jillian squared her shoulders and opened the door.

As they stepped into the sunlight, JR's eyes widened. Rafe gave him a terse nod, unpenned Calvin, then beat a hasty retreat out of there.

10

"In the almost three weeks since I was last here, Georgia sure has grown," Jillian marveled, gazing at the infant nursing at her mother's breast.

"She's gained almost two pounds and a third of an inch in length," Shannon proudly shared. "Which puts her in the eighty-fifth percentile for all babies her age." She smoothed her hand over the little round head. "Isn't she something?"

Her tender smile tugged at Jillian's heart and made her want a baby of her own all the more.

"That's some sigh," Shannon said. "The second you walked in, I sensed something was off. What's wrong?"

"You know me so well." Jillian crossed her legs and laced her fingers in her lap. Eager to spill her troubles, she got right to the point. "It's Rafe."

"Hunky firefighter Rafe? The one who isn't your type?" Shannon arched her eyebrows.

"All right. I'm attracted to him. That doesn't mean he's the man for me. Although he's such a great guy. I mean, he got JR a job." On the phone last week, she'd told Shannon about her brother's temporary employment and had shared that she'd given him a deadline to move out. "This is his first day at work, and he actually whistled as he left this morning."

"That's a nice change. Back to you and Rafe. You were saying he's not the man for you, but..." Her eyebrows arched in question.

"There's some other stuff."

"Such as?"

"We have this amazing chemistry." Jillian's cheeks grew warm, and she knew she was blushing.

"You two are having sex? Get out of town!"

"Actually, no, but we have discussed it." Last week, after engaging in some of the most arousing foreplay of Jillian's life. Since then, despite continually reminding herself Rafe was all wrong for her, her longing for him had only grown.

"We both agreed it shouldn't happen," she explained. "From now on, we're going to avoid each other, but if, for some reason, we happen to meet, we'll make sure other people are around. Because when the two of us are alone together..." Searching for the right way to describe the intense feelings between them, Jillian paused. "It's dangerous."

"The attraction is that strong?"

Miserable, Jillian nodded. "More powerful than anything else I've experienced."

"You're not exactly jumping for joy. Maybe you don't want to stay away from him."

"No, but if I'm going to find a man who wants to

settle down and start a family, it's for the best. May I burp Georgia?"

"Be my guest." While Jillian coaxed out a burp, the conversation focused on the infant.

Then Shannon changed her diaper and laid her in the crib. As soon as Jillian and her friend returned to the living room, Shannon picked up where they'd left off. "When you talk about Rafe, your whole face changes. Are you in love with him?"

Over the past week, Jillian had mulled over that very question. "I can't afford to fall for him, Shannon. It's lust. I think." She laughed without a shred of humor. "How's that for a confusing answer?"

"You sound mixed-up, all right. Speaking of sex, my doctor says Asher and I have to wait a few more weeks before we can have it again. Asher is getting antsy, but between my stitches and feeding this little peanut every three hours, making love isn't exactly a priority right now."

"Well, I fantasize about it with Rafe all the time." Jillian had even enjoyed a few feverish dreams. "I wish I could stop thinking about him. He's getting in the way of finding my Mr. Right."

Shannon gave her a searching look. "Would it be so terrible to indulge yourself without falling for him? You know, to get him out of your system. Then you'll be able to move on."

"Hmm..." Jillian considered that. Since breaking up with Doug, she'd been involved with several men, without losing her heart to any of them. "That's tempting, but Rafe and I haven't spoken since we agreed to steer clear of each other a week ago." Seven whole days of aching for him. "For all I know, he's already moved on."

"There's only one way to find out—ask the man."

"Chase after him? That's not my style. If he's moved on, I'm going to do the same."

Wednesday dawned cool and sunny, perfect for working outside. After lunch, Rafe drove toward his property. JR and Zach had started clearing the site of his future home this morning, and he wanted a visual of their progress.

Zach's shiny red truck, easily identified by the white "Zach's Tree and Root Removal" ad on the door, sat parked in the dirt area closest to the property. After parking the Beemer beside it and grabbing three cans of chilled pop from the passenger seat, Rafe strode down the hill. Trees blocked his view of the work area, but he heard the buzz of the chainsaw and smelled the scent of freshly cut wood.

Abruptly, the noise cut off. Zach called out words Rafe couldn't make out, and a loud crash shattered the brief silence and shook the ground. Moments later, Rafe found Zach and JR standing near the fifteen-foot ginkgo they'd felled. Both men wore safety glasses and heavy gloves. Zach, shorter and stockier than JR and a good thirty years older, pointed the chainsaw at the prone tree and said something, his ponytailed hair swishing across his back.

"How's it going?" Rafe called out, handing each man a pop.

"Not bad." Zach opened his drink. "Thanks, man."

"Yeah, thanks." JR mopped the sweat from his face with the hem of his T-shirt then touched the icy can to his forehead. "This is hard work."

"You ain't seen nothin' yet," Zach drawled. "We're only halfway through the first day."

In contrast to JR, the older man had barely broken a sweat. Rafe figured the kid could benefit from using some of the mental tools his father had taught him. "Okay if I borrow JR for a minute?" he asked.

"No problem." Zach drained his pop and then crumpled the empty can in his hand. "Toss this for me, JR. I'm going to start cutting up that gingko."

After JR deposited the can in a trash bag, Rafe gestured at a relatively level patch of grass. "Let's sit." He waited until they were both on the ground before he spoke again. "You doing okay?"

"Yeah." Wearing a suspicious frown, JR eyed him. "Why?"

"No reason."

"Did Jill ask you to check on me?" JR tipped up his head back and guzzled the stuff.

Rafe hadn't seen or spoken to her in days—for all the good that did. He thought about her constantly. Being with her, talking and teasing each other, fooling around... She drove him nuts.

"No," he said gruffly. "But you do seem tired. I know a trick or two that can help. Have you heard of mindful observation?"

"Mindful what?"

The chainsaw roared into action, and Rafe had to raise his voice over the noise. "Observation. It's a technique my father taught me. When the going gets tough and you want to quit—"

"Who said anything about quitting?"

Talk about a hair-trigger defensive attitude. "I'm trying to tell you about the power of mindful observation. I use it whenever I want to quit before I should. Say I'm running and my legs are killing me and my brain is screaming at me to forget running and walk instead. The first thing I do is notice those feelings. Then I focus on something else—my heartbeat, my breathing, the rhythm of my footsteps. When done right, I can push through the pain and stop thinking about giving up."

JR listened intently. "Does that really work?"

"Now it does, but it took practice a lot to get here. If you want to try the technique, I'll give you some pointers."

The kid glanced at the ground. "Maybe later."

He wasn't interested. Having been there himself, Rafe understood. "Say the word, and we'll practice. Anytime."

JR shrugged and finished his drink. He needed to go help Zach, but, first, Rafe needed information.

"Did Chelsea get the job she applied for?" he asked.

"We don't think so. It's been a week, and she hasn't heard anything."

"That's too bad," Rafe said, knowing Jillian wanted them both working and in their own place.

"Chelsea's going to help Jill at the art fair

next month. She'll earn a little money. My sister's been working like a crazed woman. She says she needs to make even more pottery, but she already has too many pieces to fit in her car. She had to ask a friend to drive her and her stuff to the Medford Fairgrounds in his pickup."

At the thought of some guy interested enough in Jillian to drive her a hundred eighty miles round-trip, Rafe's eyes narrowed. He didn't want to get involved with her himself, but he didn't want anyone else to, either. Go figure.

He schooled his expression into indifference. "Which friend is that?"

"A guy named Miller. She buys her clay and glazes from him."

"Are they dating?"

"Nah, they're only friends." JR's eyes took on a canny gleam. "You're interested in my sister. I saw the way you stared at her when you two came out of her studio last week."

Rafe gave him the stony look that shut people up. "So far, she's taught two pottery classes. How's that going?"

"The second one ran late. She was dragging yesterday."

"Did you help her clean up after?"

"Chelsea did."

"I thought you agreed to do that."

"Get off my case."

Rafe ignored the belligerent tone. "You made a deal with your sister to help clean up after her classes."

"Chelsea told me to relax before I started this job, and Jill okayed that."

Rafe let it go. "So Jillian was tired. Hard work will do that to a person. I suspect you'll be pretty worn out tonight, too. You'll probably fall asleep early."

"If Chelsea will leave me alone. Now that she's pregnant, she wants sex all the time."

JR didn't look too upset about that. Lucky bastard.

Rafe imagined Jillian in his bed, hungry and eager. His body stirred.

Cutting off his thoughts, he pushed to his feet and brushed off his backside. "I need to leave and you should get back to helping Zach."

JR nodded and also stood. "See you whenever."

11

Cupping a mug of tea, Jillian ran a practiced eye over the motley assortment of pots her students had made in their second class. Not half-bad for novice potters. During last night's class, they'd carefully filed off the rough edges and then applied glazes. By tomorrow, the pieces would be ready for a second kiln firing.

Time kept flying by. Could this really be the last day of March, with only one class left?

Jillian had enjoyed every minute of teaching. Her students were determined to do their best, but also able to laugh at themselves. All six talked about signing up for the advanced class in May. Yay!

Her thoughts turned to the art festival, which was only two and a half weeks away, and that satisfied feeling turned into panic. She wasn't ready, didn't have enough inventory yet. But she wasn't clear where to concentrate her efforts.

She sat down at the table and studied her art festival inventory spreadsheet. As she made a list of supplies she needed, Pooh, penned outside, began to bark. Not the usual *A squirrel just ran by* bark. This was a sharp, worried sound. Puzzled, Jillian wandered outside. Pooh stood at the fence with her nose pointed toward the house. She didn't even swivel her head around to glance at Jillian.

Something was wrong.

"What's the matter, girl?" Jillian asked, frowning as she entered the fenced area. The dog dashed to her side then, whined and raced back to the side of the fence facing the house.

"Don't you dare run off," Jillian warned, opening the gate.

Pooh went straight for the back door. JR was at work—his sixth day on the job. He was still showing up every morning and staying there until dinnertime, which was something to marvel over.

Chelsea had struck out. She'd applied for more than a few jobs, but the pregnancy seemed to be working against her. This morning, she'd gotten up to see JR off and then gone back to bed to sleep a little more. She was still inside.

Filled with foreboding, Jillian let Pooh inside. The dog dashed through the kitchen, toward the bathroom.

"Chelsea?" Jillian called out, following along.

"In here," the girl answered in a small, frightened voice.

Jillian found her sitting on the bathroom floor with her back against the wall, blubbering. Pooh whimpered, trotted to her side, and licked her face.

Worried, Jillian, squatted down beside her. "What's wrong?"

"When I used the toilet..." Chelsea paused and gulped. "There was blood. I think I might be having a miscarriage." Tears spilled from her eyes.

Although alarmed, Jillian forced an easy tone. "You don't know that. It could be nothing."

"But I'm bleeding! I'm only twelve weeks pregnant. I don't want to lose my baby."

Praying she wouldn't, Jillian brushed Chelsea's bangs out of her eyes. "You should lie down."

She helped the girl to the living room sofa. After making her comfortable and covering her with a fleece throw, she laid her hand on Chelsea's cool forehead, the only thing she could think of. "You don't seem to have a fever, which is good," she said. "Now, try to relax while I call 911."

When she finished the call, she thought about alerting JR. The trouble was, he didn't have a phone. Zach did, but she didn't know the number. She wasn't about to leave Chelsea to get her brother.

While pretending to be calm, in her mind, she railed at him. *Darn you, JR, you have a baby on the way! Can't you take more responsibility and look harder for a permanent job, so you can get cell phones for you and Chelsea?*

In less than ten minutes, sirens wailed through the air and the aid car pulled up. Talk about fast. They must have raced to get here.

Jillian had met the three gorgeous paramedics who tromped into the house before—Ethan, Gus, and Rafe. She'd never felt so relieved to see them. Especially Rafe.

All business, he nodded a grave hello. "Where is

she?"

For some reason, the cool Jillian had managed to maintain crumpled. She teared up. "In the living room."

"Hey, now." He gently squeezed her shoulder. "She's in good hands."

Jillian forced a smile. Not wanting to get in the way, she hovered in the hallway outside the living room, hugging Pooh while the men questioned Chelsea and examined her. A moment later, Rafe beckoned her to follow him into the kitchen.

"Well?" she asked in a low voice.

"She seems okay, but to be on the safe side, we think she should go to the hospital and get checked out. You could drive her, but because our vehicle is equipped with a stretcher and other equipment, she asked us to take her. In case she starts bleeding again—or something else."

"Is that a possibility?"

"Probably not, but you never know. You should alert her doctor."

"Right away. What about JR?" Jillian couldn't help curling her lip. "He still doesn't have a phone. Do you have Zach's number?"

"Yeah." Rafe gave it to her. "After you call, swing by and pick him up. Then meet us at the hospital."

"How will we find you?"

"I'll let you know where we are."

~

SHORTLY AFTER RAFE and his coworkers delivered Chelsea to the ER, Jillian and her brother arrived.

JR went straight to Chelsea's exam room, while Rafe, Ethan, and Gus stayed in the crowded waiting area with Jillian.

With her arms around her waist and her teeth doing double time on her bottom lip, she radiated worry.

"You doing okay?" Rafe asked, peering into her face.

"Not really. If Chelsea loses that baby..." She closed her eyes for a moment, obviously struggling for control, and then went back to biting her lip.

He hated seeing her this upset. "Don't do this to yourself, Jillian, when there's no reason to go there." He gently unwrapped her arms, grasped one of her cold hands, and gave it a reassuring squeeze. "Chelsea should be fine."

"Please, God," Jillian murmured, holding on tight. "I'm beyond grateful that you, Gus, and Ethan came to the house and then got her here so fast."

She hiccupped, a sound that could have been a strangled laugh or a sob. "It seems all I ever do is thank you."

She wouldn't be so grateful if she knew how bad Rafe wanted her. Even now, which proved what a dog he was. He let go of her hand.

"Don't you have to get back to the station?" she asked.

He didn't want to leave her alone just yet. "We'll hang with you until we find out what the doctor says. It shouldn't be much longer."

"Do you usually wait around with patients you bring to the hospital?"

"Depends on the situation and the patient. We

know you, which makes a difference. How about a pop or snack from the vending machine?"

Jillian shook her head. "I couldn't eat or drink anything. Tell me, how is JR doing?"

"According to Zach, he shows up on time and puts in a full day. But clearing the land has been rough and slow-going. It could take him and Zach longer than we figured to finish the job."

"He complains a lot about that."

Rafe could just imagine. "I offered to share a focusing trick my dad taught me to make tough work easier. I use it to get through anything physically challenging, both on and off the job. He wasn't interested."

"My brother always has been his own worst enemy. All I know is, when he finishes clearing your land, he'd better look hard for permanent work, or I swear, I'll wring his stubborn neck."

"You gave him a deadline," Rafe reminded her.

"Yes, but now..." She cast an anxious look toward the swinging doors leading to the ER exam rooms.

"Let's wait and see what the doctor says."

She nodded and put her hand on his arm. "If you hear about work JR might be qualified for, will you let him know?"

If JR continued to show up and put in a full day's work, Rafe figured Zach would add him to the stable of extra hands he relied on for various jobs. That wouldn't be full-time, though, and the kid needed a steady paycheck. He nodded. "Of course."

The swinging doors opened, and a middle-age nurse with a warm smile approached Jillian. "Your brother and Chelsea wanted me to let you know she's going to be fine."

"Thank goodness." Jillian sank against Rafe.

"I told you." He smiled and, without thinking, put his arm around her and pulled her close.

"What happened?" she asked the nurse.

"It's not unusual for a pregnant woman to experience intermittent bleeding, especially during the first trimester. Still, you're always wise to get checked out, in case it's something serious. If the bleeding recurs, or if she experiences cramping and bleeding together, she should come right back. Chelsea and JR are aware of this."

"Good to know," Jillian said. "Should she do anything special? Maybe stay off her feet?"

"That won't be necessary. She's already scheduled an appointment with her OB for tomorrow. She'll find out then if the doctor wants her to limit her activities. She should be out in a little while."

The nurse retraced her steps through the swinging doors. Time for Rafe and his coworkers to go, too.

"I'll check in with you soon," Rafe said.

"If you want."

Unable to stop himself, he tipped up her chin. "I want."

His nosy crewmates and everyone else in the waiting area were staring. Even so, he kissed her.

Jillian let out a soft sigh, and it was all he could do to tear himself away.

"Rest easy. Tell JR to take the rest of the day off and spend it with Chelsea—I already cleared it with Zach." He nodded at his buds. "Let's go."

12

While Max, that night's chef, banged the pots and pans around, Rafe and the rest of the firefighters tromped down to the apparatus bay.

In a small cleanup room off the main area, Gus and Ethan scrubbed and sterilized the equipment they'd used on their most recent patient, an eight-year-old boy who'd fallen on the playground and gashed his leg. Rafe got busy sanitizing the bed in the aid car and restocking depleted supplies. Having dealt with a nasty fire at an apartment building earlier, Adam and some of the guys on firefighter duty put the two fire trucks to rights.

Rafe finished his task and checked his watch. "Five minutes till we eat."

All meals were taken at specific times, with dinner served promptly at eighteen hundred hours. With the exception of fire and paramedic calls, the captain required everyone on duty to show up on time, period. After washing up, Rafe and the other guys climbed the stairs to the second floor.

Soon they were seated and passing around mega bowls of salad, hot rolls, steaming green beans, and Max's cheesy chicken casserole, a tried-and-true favorite.

Everyone dug in, and the room went quiet. Rafe was working his way through second helpings when Adam elbowed him.

"I hear you kissed Jillian in the ER this afternoon. Wish I could have seen that."

Rafe had been expecting this and had decided to play it cool. He shrugged. "She was upset and needed reassuring."

Gus snickered. "You did a whole lot more than that. One little kiss, and she melted." He shook his head. "I finally got to see the stud in action."

Around the table, men chuckled and made lewd comments. Even Captain Comings snickered.

Rafe's plan to act cool died on the spot. "Back off," he warned, scowling at the room in general.

Gus let out a good-natured laugh. "I'm only saying what I saw. Jillian's into you, and admit it, bro. You're into her. Even if she is looking to get married."

The man had him there. Rafe had never felt so inside-out, crazy in lust before. If that wasn't enough, he really cared for Jillian, more than he could ever remember liking any female. And it freaked him out.

"You're right," he admitted, scrubbing his hand over his face. "I don't what the hell to do about it."

"Follow the advice you gave me when I had the same problem with Sam," Adam said. "If you want her to be your woman, tell her."

Rafe rolled his eyes. "If I wanted to get married, that'd work. I don't."

Adam exhaled. "That's a problem, all right."

Across the table, Captain Comings eyed Rafe. "Not necessarily. People change."

Rafe frowned. "Jillian knows what she wants, and she isn't going to change her mind."

"I mean you. Do you know what you want?" The captain didn't wait for Rafe's reply. "In my twenties, I didn't have any answers, either. That was back in the dinosaur age, before any of you knew me."

Rafe and the other guys grinned. The captain was a fit forty-seven years old, not exactly ancient.

"For a long time, I was content with my fire-fighting career and bachelorhood," the captain went on, pushing his empty plate to the side and leaning on his forearms. "I enjoyed playing the field and didn't see myself any other way. Then I met Audrey. After two dates, I changed my tune. The following year, on the anniversary of the day we met, we married. Twenty-two years and three kids later, here I am—still happy and in love."

"That's great," Rafe said. "But not everyone is as lucky as you. I don't see myself with a wife and kids. Ever."

The captain spread out his hands in a yielding gesture. "If that's your choice, so be it. But if neither of you is going to change, you have to give her up."

~

THE DAY after Chelsea's scary episode, Jillian sat at the table in the studio, smoothing the rough edges on a toothbrush and soap dish set before she glazed it. As relieved as she was that all had turned out well, she was still a little shaken, and glad to have the distraction of work.

And yet, her thoughts kept straying. To the trip to the ER. To Rafe and his comforting presence. Holding her hand, reassuring her, staying at her side until they knew Chelsea was okay. His big hands, gently cradling her face, and that tender kiss...

He shouldn't have done that. She shouldn't have let him. Because now, she wanted him even more than before. More kisses, more caresses, more pleasure...

Jillian closed her eyes and relived the heaven of Rafe's hands and mouth, her longing for him so strong, if he knocked on her door this minute, she might follow Shannon's advice and make love with him, just to get rid of the aching hunger inside.

She heard Pooh's yip outside and a sound she recognized right away as Rafe's car. He'd showed up, as if she'd conjured him up through sheer desire.

Her heart lifted, and certain parts of her anatomy quivered, and she was tempted to tell him what she wanted. Then worry took over. JR was supposed to be at Rafe's property, clearing land. What if, instead, he'd blown off work to be with Chelsea?

Jillian set her sanding tool down and stepped outside, into another bright, sunny day.

Wearing aviator glasses, Rafe was hunkered down at the fence, greeting Pooh. His green T-shirt stretched across his shoulders and clung to his muscled biceps. An admiring breath stuttered from Jillian's lips, and certain body parts began to hum.

Frowning at the thought, she shaded her eyes against the sun. "What are you doing here?"

What was he doing here? Rafe wondered. Because he agreed with the captain's advice that he needed to forget Jillian for good.

He cleared his throat. "I wanted to check on Chelsea, and uh...see how you're doing."

"She's at the doctor's right now. On the way, she dropped JR at your property. At least, she was supposed to."

"I stopped there before coming here," Rafe said. "He's there."

Jillian's exhale was pure relief. Then frown lines cut across her forehead. "Did you talk to him? Because if you did, then you already know Chelsea's fine."

Busted. "Hell, Jillian. Never mind." Rafe shoved his hands in his pockets, shifted his weight and turned to leave.

"Why did you kiss me at the hospital?"

He swung back toward her. Not about to lie, he told her. "Because I couldn't help myself."

"I know." Both hands combed through her hair. "I'm driving myself crazy thinking about us."

"Us?" He whipped off his shades.

"You know—together." Although she blushed, she held his gaze.

"Making love," he clarified.

A charged look passed between them, so palpable, the air shimmered with hunger and heat.

His feelings tumbled out in a blunt statement. "I want you, Jillian."

"It's the wanting I think about, Rafe. All the time, no matter how busy I am or what I do to block it. That kiss yesterday only made my desire more intense." She swallowed audibly.

Her frankness staggered him. He couldn't recall any other female in his life ever being so forthright, had never met a woman like her. While he wondered at that, she blew him away with more.

"When the longing is this strong, attempting to fight it is pointless."

Didn't he know it. "You're thinking if we make love, the problem will go away."

"Do you have a better idea?"

He shook his head.

"Well, then."

As bad as he wanted what she offered, he questioned the wisdom of moving ahead. Not without a reminder. "Remember, I'm not—"

"The marrying kind. I would never ask for a marriage proposal or even a commitment. I just want to move past this...whatever this feeling is, and get on with my life."

Rafe was on board with that. "Where and when?"

"As soon as possible."

"How about today."

"That takes care of the when. As for where, the too-short, lumpy sofa in my studio is out, and with Chelsea due back at any time..."

"Not much privacy," Rafe agreed. "My place, then."

He didn't usually invite a woman into his own bed, but these were special circumstances.

"Where do you live?" she asked.

"On the north side of town. Give me your phone."

His name and cell number were already stored under contacts. He added his address.

"What time do you want me?"

"All the time," he growled without masking his hunger.

The desire on her face almost did him in. He stepped back. "I just got off shift and haven't been home in two days. I need to collect Calvin from the dog sitter's and do a few things. Give me an hour."

13

Some ninety minutes later, Jillian turned onto Rafe's street. He lived in an upscale area of landscaped yards and well-maintained homes, she noted in an effort to settle a bad case of nerves. It didn't work. By the time she found his house and pulled up the concrete driveway, she began to question herself.

Did she really want to do this?

More than anything. The only catch was, deep down, in a place she kept hidden from everyone, often even herself, she feared her feelings for Rafe went beyond strong physical need.

Refusing to think about that, she followed the stone walkway toward his two-story brick house. As she drew closer, she heard Calvin's excited woof from inside. Moments after she rang the doorbell, Rafe answered. Barefoot, and wearing a black T-shirt and jeans.

"Did you have any trouble finding the house?" he asked after she greeted the dog in the large, tiled entry.

"None at all. This is a nice neighborhood. Why would you want to leave it and move out to the boonies?"

"For starters, I don't own this place."

A house as classy as this—a rental? She couldn't hide her surprise.

"A guy's gotta live someplace while he waits for the right plot of land for his home." He ushered her into a carpeted living room with masculine furniture and bold paintings on white walls. "I need to let Calvin out. Can I get you something to drink?"

"Do you have tea?"

"Picked up some on my way home, just for you."

Aw. How sweet.

"Sit tight while I make it."

While she waited for him to return, she rambled around the room. Out the window facing the backyard, she could see Calvin racing around the large fenced area and dog house. The fireplace mantel contained a picture of a man who had to be Rafe's father and a skinny preteen boy who was obviously Rafe. Standing near a basketball hoop, their matching dimples flashing, Rafe looked poised to shoot the basketball, while his father's arms raised in an attempt to block him. There were no other photos.

Rafe returned to the room with tea and a coffee for himself.

"That's a great picture of you and your dad," she said as he directed her toward a massive sofa. She sat down, sliding across the buttery brown leather.

Rafe joined her. Not so close they touched, but close enough to feel his warmth.

"I was eleven and finally adjusting to life with a man who believed in structure and discipline."

"You didn't butt heads?" Jillian asked, thinking of her own father.

"A lot that first year. Then, not so much."

In the silence that fell between them, she gulped tea and wracked her brain for something else to talk about. "When you stopped by earlier, I thought maybe JR had skipped work," she finally said.

"With the wages he's earning, not a chance."

Jillian nodded and searched for another topic. "How are the house plans coming along?"

"I'll find out tomorrow, when I meet with Sonia to review the preliminary blueprints."

"Are you excited?"

"You know it. I gave her a detailed list of the things I wanted, and it'll be good to see what she came up with."

Of course, he would.

Jillian had drained her mug. She shifted uncomfortably, causing the leather to creak.

Rafe squinted at her. "You okay?"

"I'm a little nervous," she admitted.

"You changed your mind." His expression was impossible to read.

"No."

Visibly relieved, he flashed his dimples. "Let me help you relax."

"It's too early for alcohol."

"I know something much better. Turn your back to me."

He pushed her hair to the side and gave her the

best shoulder and neck massage of her life.

She moaned. "Oh, you're good."

"This is just a prelude to what happens next."

His words and the low, slightly hoarse timbre of his voice wreaked havoc inside her. Every atom in her body tensed impatiently. To her frustration, he continued the massage without going near her breasts or down lower.

"Still nervous?" he asked.

"Not anymore. Maybe I should take off my top. You know, so you can really get at the kinks." Although, thanks to Rafe, her muscles felt like melted butter.

"I've been waiting for you to say that."

He was letting her set the pace, she realized. Enjoying her power, she turned to face him and slowly pulled her V-neck shirt over her head. Earlier, she'd showered and changed into her best bra, a violet, lacy demi that pushed her breasts together and gave her some cleavage.

Rafe's eyes went dark and hot, which she'd anticipated. "Shall I leave this on, or take it off?" she asked in her best seductive voice.

"Take it off."

She reached behind her to do just that, but Rafe stopped her. "Let me."

Moving in back of her, he made quick work of the clasp. For a man with such large hands, he certainly was skilled at unfastening the itty-bitty hooks.

But then, he'd had plenty of practice with multiple women.

Not about to dwell on that now, Jillian pushed the thought from her mind.

"I think I'll get rid of my shirt, too," he said, still at her back.

She heard the rustle then watched as the shirt sailed past her and dropped to the carpet. He pulled her against his hard chest, held her close and from behind, cupped her breasts.

At last. Pleasure rippled through her, and she stopped thinking, period.

Soon, desperate to kiss him, she pivoted in his arms. On her knees, she brushed her hands through the smattering of soft hair on his chest. Flicked her tongue over his nipples.

Groaning, Rafe lifted her onto his lap and kissed her savagely. Deep, tongue-jousting kisses she wanted never to end.

After some time, or maybe only a minute—she wasn't sure—he broke contact. "If we're going to make it to my bed, and that's where I want to make love with you, we need to go upstairs."

Not minding at all that he'd taken charge, Jillian nodded.

"Take off your boots and socks then wrap your legs around me," he directed.

As soon as she did, he cupped her behind, pushed to his feet as if she weighed nothing, and carried her easily toward the stairs.

They didn't get far before he paused to kiss her. Dizzy with desire and love—no, she was not falling for him—Jillian shifted restlessly in his arms.

"Patience," he growled against her lips.

"I'm running out of that."

Rafe continued up the stairs with no more stops. On the second floor, he strode forward at a rapid clip, straight into the bedroom. Jillian caught a glimpse of gray carpeting, heavy curtains pulled for privacy, and a dark-wood headboard.

He set her down. Watching each other, they unzipped their jeans and shed the rest of their clothing. Finally naked, they stood facing each other.

Rafe was well-endowed and aroused, glorious to look at.

"You are so beautiful." His scorching gaze roved over her, igniting her everywhere. "Come here."

He wrapped her in his arms and simply held her. At first she thought she was the one trembling. But, no. "You're shaking," she said.

"Because I want you so much." Taking her hand, he led her to his bed.

The covers were already turned back in welcome. He pulled her down with him onto satiny sheets. His mouth and hands went everywhere, stroking, licking, consuming...

On fire, she climaxed. Not once but twice before he allowed her to touch him.

Jillian pushed him onto his back and slowly ran her hands down his gorgeous abs, his flat belly. As she moved lower, Rafe hissed in a breath. She circled his rigid length and explored, marveling over the taut, velvety skin.

Moaning, he raised his hips and pushed into her hand. When she tried to put her mouth on him, he stopped her. "I'm on the edge here," he warned. "When I lose control, it will be inside you."

Jillian was ready. "Where do you keep the condoms?"

"In the bedside table drawer."

He started to sit up, but she shook her head. "Stay where you are."

She found the foil packets. There were at least a half dozen.

She couldn't help wondering about the women he'd brought here before her and those who would take her place later. But thinking about that hurt, and she made herself stop.

Rafe tore the condom open and sheathed himself. He reached for her.

"Uh-uh. On your back again, firefighter," she ordered.

His eyes glittering dangerously, he complied.

Straddling his hard body, she inched down until he was buried inside her. Groaning, he gripped her hips and raised up, pushing even deeper, until she was certain he touched her very soul.

Her body pulsed as the delicious tension low in her body coiled tighter and tighter. She began to shudder with pleasure. Rafe urged her to move faster, until they climaxed together. One long, shuddering cataclysm obliterating all but the two of them, joined as one.

When it finally ended, Jillian collapsed on his chest. They were both sweaty and breathing hard.

Her body was replete and spent, and her heart full to bursting. It had found Mr. Right. Unfortunately for her, Rafe wasn't her Mr. Right. He didn't want to be.

What they'd intended to be sex and only sex, a way to get out of each other's systems, had become much, much more. For her, anyway.

What to do? Hiding her feelings seemed the safest route. Jillian had never been good at that, but for her sake, she must.

~

BLOWN AWAY by the best sex of his life, Rafe pulled Jillian closer. "That was off the charts."

"We were pretty amazing."

He tipped up her chin and kissed her sexy mouth. "Give me time to recover. Then we'll do it again."

For some reason, she tensed up and wouldn't meet his eyes. "Better not. I should probably get home."

Caught off guard, he frowned. "Do you have something scheduled?"

"Work. I'm a little behind on my inventory for the art festival." She still wouldn't look at him.

His gut twisted. "Something's wrong."

"It's just... We said one time."

"Maybe once isn't enough."

Not for him. By Jillian's passionate response and enthusiastic participation, she'd liked having sex with him. A lot. He nuzzled the sensitive crook of her shoulder, pleased when she moaned and tilted her head to the side to give him better access. She wanted more, too.

"What if I want to spend the rest of the day and

all night in bed with you?" he said, moving to kiss her lips again.

"I can't, Rafe." Pulling out of his arms and taking the blanket with her, she scrambled out of bed.

Confused, he sat up. "I don't understand. You enjoyed making love as much as I did."

In the process of wrapping the king-size cover around herself—no easy task—she glanced at him. "That's true." She bit her lip then looked away.

Rafe stood and helped her secure the blanket under her arms. She smelled good, a combination of their lovemaking and her special woman scent.

"You're hiding something," he said, going commando as he stepped into his jeans. "Spit it out, Jillian."

"I shouldn't."

He got into her face, and she had to meet his eyes. "Talk to me."

She muttered something about being a lousy liar then sighed. "Since you won't let this go... I'm afraid to have sex with you again."

Her words totally surprised him. "You're afraid of me?" He scoffed. "When you screamed my name during your three orgasms, you sure didn't seem scared."

This time, she looked directly at him. "I'm not talking about you, Rafe. As big and powerful as you are, I know you'd never hurt me. You were passionate, considerate, tender—the best lover I could ever want. I loved what we did. Every second of it."

"So what's the deal?"

She cleared her throat a couple of times, as if

the next words were difficult to get out. "This is about me and my feelings for you."

He didn't like the sound of that. "You said they were purely sexual."

"I wanted them to be."

Aw, hell, she'd fallen for him. He'd never guessed. Or maybe he'd wanted her so much, he'd turned a blind eye. Either way, this was not good.

Rafe scrubbed his hand over his face and fumbled for the right words. "You know I like you a lot. But for me, that's as far as it goes."

"And it's okay." Still clutching the blanket tightly around her, she retrieved her jeans and panties from the carpet. "If you don't mind bringing me my bra, shirt, ankle boots, and socks, I'll get dressed in your bathroom."

In the living room downstairs, his mind reeling, Rafe tugged his T-shirt over his head, collected Jillian's things, and returned to the bedroom. The bathroom door was closed. He knocked. "I have your things."

The door opened wide enough for her to snatch her stuff before it clicked shut again.

Rafe straightened and remade the bed. Sitting on the edge of it, he smacked his forehead with his palm. Dammit, he hadn't wanted this awkwardness between them. He certainly hadn't intended to hurt her.

That's what he got for letting his crazy lust for her color his judgment.

He figured she wouldn't want to see him again. He wasn't happy about that, but the way things stood, keeping a distance seemed the best option.

Still, as future neighbors, they were bound to run into each other. Would they be able to exchange hellos without suffering through uncomfortable stiffness and tension?

Rafe had no idea. He only knew he'd screwed up, big-time.

At least she wouldn't have to pretend she didn't have deep feelings for Rafe, Jillian consoled herself as she dressed in his bathroom.

Standing at the mirror to smooth her hair, she couldn't help noting her pink, slightly swollen lips and flushed skin. The image of a thoroughly loved woman.

In the physical sense, she was.

Rafe was waiting for her. Time to quit hiding in here, go out and face him. Ignoring the painful ache in her chest, she opened the door and re-entered the bedroom.

He sprang up from the bed, which, of course, he'd made. The tightly tucked sheets and blanket erased any signs of their passionate afternoon.

He scratched the back of his neck. "I don't know what to say. Don't ask me to apologize for what happened. I'm not sorry."

Neither was Jillian. Making love with Rafe had opened her eyes to the truth—she'd loved him long before today. "You didn't force me to come here, Rafe. I chose to. There's nothing more to add, except good-bye."

"I don't like leaving things this way."

Hating the concern in his eyes, she forced a brave smile. "I really am okay."

After a long, searching look, he gave a terse nod. Jillian headed downstairs, leaving him to follow or not. Of course, he did.

She picked her purse up from the living room floor and searched for the car key for an embarrassingly long time before she finally found it.

"Drive safe," Rafe said at the front door.

"I will."

She made her way down the walkway, toward her car. The sinking sun cast long shadows over the new spring grass.

Rafe stayed in the doorway, watching as she slid into the driver's seat, started the car, and backed away, out of the driveway and his life.

THURSDAY AFTERNOON, Sonia ushered Rafe into her plush office with a big smile. "I can't wait to show you the preliminary blueprints for the house. How about a cup of coffee and a doughnut?"

After Rafe accepted both, she pulled an extra chair up beside hers and motioned for him to join her at the computer. As he sat down, he caught a whiff of her perfume, a seductive scent meant to stir a man's interest. He wasn't interested.

He was still smarting from what had happened

after yesterday's phenomenal sex. The fallout from hell.

It had been almost twenty-four hours since Jillian had left his place, and he felt worse than before. He wondered about Jillian, and whether it was this bad for her.

"Let's start with the second story." Sonia tapped the keyboard. "First, a bird's-eye view of the master suite. You'll notice that I incorporated the home office on the other side of the master bath, exactly as you requested."

Rafe nodded. She switched to a more detailed outline of the suite. "The bedroom, bathroom, and office all face Guff's Lake for a stunning view." She pointed out the floor-to-ceiling windows in each room. "And, of course, the deck off the bedroom allows you to sit outside and enjoy coffee or a meal while you take in the view."

She'd done an excellent job incorporating Rafe's ideas, yet he couldn't muster up much enthusiasm. "It's nice," he said.

"Just nice?" Sonia gave him a funny look. "You don't like it."

Pulling himself together, Rafe smiled. "You've done an excellent job. Show me more."

~

At breakfast Thursday morning, JR frowned. "What's with you today, Jill?" Chelsea was still asleep. "You seem down."

No kidding. Refusing to let her stupidity get the best of her, Jillian stretched and yawned, as if all was right with the world. "I stayed up late last night, working. I'm tired."

"You think you're tired... My whole body aches. I wish I could stay home and rest today, but Zach and Rafe want the job finished as soon as possible. That means I'll be working Saturday and probably Sunday."

"Those mind-focus tricks he wanted to teach you would probably help," Jillian pointed out. "But you wouldn't even let him show you how to use them."

"He told you about that? You asked him to keep an eye on me, didn't you?" JR's eyes narrowed. "I don't like you spying on me."

In no mood for her brother's prickly ways, Jillian rolled her eyes. "Rafe wouldn't spy on you, and I would never ask him to." From now on, they wouldn't be talking about anything, period. "Don't forget to ask Zach for a permanent job."

A scowl darkened JR's face. "Like I haven't thought about that. I know you're disappointed in me."

"Oh, stop it. I am not."

The only person disappointing Jillian was her own foolish self, for making love with Rafe when she knew better. She tried for a friendlier tone. "I could use more tea. Do you have time for another cup of coffee?"

"Not really, but I'll take some in my thermos. I'm no slacker, Jill, so lay off. And stop giving me dirty looks."

"Dirty looks?" Jillian's temper snapped. "Quit

being so defensive. I'm not Dad, and not everything is about you!"

Her brother jerked back as if she'd slapped him, and she knew her angry tone had shocked him.

"You don't have to yell," he said.

"Then get off my case."

"You sound like me." He crossed his eyes and stuck out his tongue, his way of trying to make her laugh. She couldn't quite summon a smile.

He started to say something else, but she cut him off. "Whatever it is, I don't want to hear it."

His expression turned stony. "Keep your damn coffee. I'm out of here."

15

Saturday dawned another warm, dry day, the tenth in a row without rain. Already the earth was hard and dusty—not a good omen for the upcoming summer and fire season, but a good day for a run.

Mid-morning, Rafe and Calvin met Hank and Gus on the dirt patch near his land. Although he didn't see Zach's truck, he heard a bulldozer.

"I haven't seen my building site since Sunday," he said. "Let's head down there and check it out."

Hank shrugged. "Sounds good."

"And then loop around and pass by Jillian's, like we did last time," Gus added.

Rafe had no intention of going near her place. "You haven't seen the other side of my property," he said as he leashed Calvin. "Why don't we head there instead?"

His buds shared a look. "So you decided to leave Jillian alone," Hank said.

Not about to explain, Rafe whistled, signaling his dog to run. Calvin yipped, and they took off.

As soon as Rafe's two pals caught up, Gus said, "You had sex with her."

He and Hank grinned, but one look at Rafe's face and their smiles vanished.

Gus was starting to breathe hard now, but that didn't stop his nosy mouth from moving. "So you struck out."

Rafe ran for several minutes before replying. "Let's say, she's falling for me."

Barely winded, Hank shrugged. "Sooner or later, they all do."

"Not if I can help it."

Rafe's shins were beginning to burn. Within moments, the pain grew too intense to ignore. He tried mindful observation, but he was too distracted to focus. Swearing, he tugged on Calvin's leash and slowed to a walk. "Shin splints," he grumbled.

Hank and Gus followed suit, Gus shaking his head. "That's what you get for taking off without stretching. What's your plan?"

"Like I told you, check on JR and then run through the rest of the property."

"I mean, about Jillian."

"Follow the captain's advice."

"You should have done that before you hopped into the sack with her."

Rafe glared at the fool.

Unperturbed, Gus calmly eyed him. "You're in one hell of a shitty mood."

Rafe had never felt so rotten in his life, as if darkness shrouded the world.

Hank frowned. "Out with it, man. What'd she do, screw you over somehow?"

"She wouldn't do that. The thing is, I really like her."

"So you said a couple weeks ago." For a moment, Gus looked pensive. Then the know-it-all hooted. "Well, well. This is something I never thought to see—Rafe Donato in love."

"You're full of crap." Ignoring his smarting shins, Rafe whistled to Calvin. They took off again.

The drone of the bulldozer had died, and suddenly the wind kicked up. Rafe smelled smoke. He ground to a halt and sniffed the air, trying to pinpoint the direction. "Do you smell that?"

"Yep. It's coming from your property—there." Gus gestured through the trees at the acrid smoke billowing upward. "Go. I'll phone it in."

Rafe, Calvin, and Hank took off at a dead run.

JILLIAN WAS MOPING over a cup of tea Saturday morning when Shannon called. "It's such a gorgeous day. Asher's taking Georgia for a walk, and I have some time to myself. For once, we can talk without any interruptions! What's going on?"

Jillian bit her lip. "How did you know I needed to talk?"

She glanced at the spare bedroom, where Chelsea was still in bed, Pooh keeping her company. To avoid the chance of her overhearing what was private, Jillian slipped out the back door.

"I hear birds," Shannon said.

Cheerful songs filled the air, already warmed by the brilliant sun. For all Jillian cared, it could have been cold and cloudy. "I stepped outside," she explained, sitting cross-legged on the stoop. "Remember a couple weeks ago, when we talked about Rafe and me?"

"You mean the sex thing?"

"Yeah. It happened."

"Ooh. When?"

"Four days ago."

"And you're just telling me? Did it work? Is he out of your system?"

"I wish."

"No big. Stay with him until he is."

"That isn't going to happen." Jillian's heavy sigh hung in the air.

"Oh, no. Did he dump you?"

"Not exactly."

"You dumped him?" Shannon sounded incredulous. "I'm confused. I get that he isn't the guy you're going to settle down with, but if you two have a good thing going..."

"I don't want to get hurt," Jillian admitted. She let out a strangled laugh. "Get hurt? I'm already there."

"So you are in love with him."

"As it turns out, I have been for weeks." A ladybug landed on her thigh. Weren't they supposed to symbolize good luck?

"What makes you so sure he doesn't love you back?"

"Because when I admitted I have feelings for him, he reminded me that he doesn't do love."

The ladybug spread her wings and flew off, taking her luck with her. Figures.

"I'm sorry."

"Hey, I knew the score going in."

"Did you at least enjoy being together?"

"A lot."

"That's something, right? Have you heard from him?"

"No, and I don't expect to. I think he got spooked by my confession."

"You never know. It's only been four days. Give him time to process the whole thing."

"Okay, but I won't hold my breath."

A siren wailed in the distance.

"I can hear that through the phone," Shannon said.

Chelsea stepped through the door in her PJs. At her side, Pooh began to howl. "I think it's coming from Rafe's property," she said, twisting her hands together.

Oh, dear God—JR. Jillian's heart stuttered in her chest. "I have to go, Shannon. I'll call you later."

16

The fire, which had started in the engine of the bulldozer, was out, leaving a nasty burnt smell in the air. After tethering Calvin to a nearby tree, Rafe, Hank, and Gus chatted with the firefighters who had taken care of the problem in short order. This crew worked a different shift, and they didn't get the chance to fraternize often.

A few yards away, Zach shook his head at the blackened equipment and chewed JR out.

As the firefighters stowed their equipment and prepared to leave, Calvin barked in excitement.

Rafe turned to see Chelsea and Jillian moving quickly across the field. As they drew closer, Chelsea ran straight for JR. As soon as she reached him, she hugged him.

Jillian hung back, but the relief on her face was hard to ignore. Once again, her brother had caused her grief.

But, then, so had Rafe.

"I'm fine," JR said, eying Zach and untangling Chelsea's arms from his waist.

With that, Jillian joined the couple and Zach. Rafe and his buds followed suit in time to hear her question. "What happened?"

JR hemmed and hawed, stumbling around the story, causing Rafe and Zach to swap incredulous looks.

"I'm not about to explain your shenanigans to your girl and your sister," JR's boss told the kid. "That's on you."

JR shifted nervously. "Uh, Zach left to scope out a future project he wants to bid on. He was gone for a while. He didn't come back until around the time the fire trucks showed up. When you're all alone, digging up tree roots is boring. I decided to spice things up a little, by putting the pedal to the metal. Like a race car driver. I was only fooling around—dozers can't go very fast."

He smiled, but when no one else did, he quickly sobered. "Somehow the front of the dozer ended up in one of the tree-root holes. I drove backward and forward and backward again, trying and trying to maneuver the thing onto level land. Instead, I created a deep rut I couldn't get out of. I must've ground the engine a little too hard. It caught fire." He grimaced. "I guess I really fuc—messed up."

Zach looked disgusted. "You can say that again."

Tight-lipped, JR scrubbed the back of his neck. "I'll get my stuff and leave."

"Stay right where you are," Rafe ordered. The kid froze. "I need to have a word with Zach. Then you and I will talk."

Hank cleared his throat. "Gus and I are going to head back, hit the showers, and grab lunch at The Rogue."

The popular Denny's-style restaurant served good food and killer curly fries. Wishing he could go with them, Rafe nodded. "Catch you later."

He motioned for Zach to follow him out of earshot from everyone else. They conferred and then rejoined JR.

"Every job has its boring moments," Zach said. "But that's no excuse for what you did. I ought to fire your ass." JR hung his head. "Would, too, if not for Rafe and the insurance I carry on the dozer."

With Rafe paying JR's wages, the tree-removal expert had little choice but to keep the kid on.

"I convinced Zach to give you another chance," Rafe said. "On two conditions. One, from now on, if you're tempted to do anything you're not supposed to, no matter what the situation, consult Zach or me. Otherwise, don't do it. And, two, I get to teach you how to do mindful observation, the mental trick I mentioned a while back."

JR started to argue, but Rafe silenced him with a look. "Do we have a deal?"

"Yes, sir."

Rafe extended his arm and shook hands with JR.

Next, JR shook Zach's hand. He frowned. "How are we supposed to work without a bulldozer?"

"A loaner is on the way," Zach explained. "While we wait, we'll deal with the tree roots you dug up earlier."

"Okay. What about the mind thing, Rafe?"

"Let's meet here tomorrow, before you start work. It'll mean an earlier morning than usual for you."

"But tomorrow's Sunday."

"Yep."

After a brief hesitation, JR gave a grudging nod. He murmured something to Chelsea, then engulfed her in a warm hug that made Rafe's heart squeeze.

JR joined Zach, and they tromped toward several massive tree roots.

"My brother has no idea how lucky he is to still have this job," Jillian told Rafe in a voice only he could hear.

"He's not a bad kid, just needs some guidance and to think things through. The focusing tools I'm going to teach him will help. I'm going to push him to go for his GED, too."

It was good to see her soft smile. For some reason, he had to swallow past a lump in his throat. "I doubt Zach will hire him again, but the owner of the construction company building the house might. I'll ask."

"You'd do that after what he pulled?"

"He's been showing up on time and works hard. That counts for something. How are you?"

Her gaze flicked away, to something over his shoulder. "Between prepping for the last pottery class and getting ready for the art festival, I'm busy. How about you?"

"Doing okay." Rafe kicked the dirt with the toe of his running shoe.

After a brief pause, Jillian brushed her hands

together, as if she'd had enough of their conversation. "I'd better get back to the studio."

With a hollow feeling Rafe didn't understand, he watched her join Chelsea at the edge of the field and walk away.

~

TEN DAYS LATER, spring was in full swing. Tooling along with the Beemer's top down at eight-fifteen a.m., Rafe smelled the flowers and heard the rumble of heavy machinery even before he pulled onto the dirt lot near his property.

Having just come off a crazy busy forty-eight-hour shift, he needed to collect Calvin from the dog-sitter's, go home and grab some Zs before heading to Adam's to help install a fence around his back yard. But Tim Marx, the builder Rafe had hired, had broken ground yesterday, and Rafe couldn't wait to take a look.

Half a dozen vehicles filled the lot, as well as the trailer Marx dubbed his traveling office. Rafe pulled to a stop and exited the Beemer. As he strode through the trees, he noted an idle grader waiting to level the area Zach and JR had cleared. Men in hard hats were stacking two-by-fours, while an excavator scooped dirt from a rapidly growing hole soon to become the foundation and basement.

At last, his own house on his own land. A dream come true that should have had him jubilant. Instead, Rafe felt even worse than when he'd met with Sonia to review the blueprints.

Chalk that up to a nasty case of woman blues.

He missed Jillian—her company, her contagious smile, her laughter. But he couldn't give her the love she wanted and deserved, and needed to keep his distance.

He walked around, searching for Tim Marx. Instead, he spotted JR. Rafe had convinced the builder to hire the kid on a trial basis. He ambled toward JR. "I'm looking for Tim."

"He's out, picking up supplies, but he should be back soon."

Rafe nodded. "How's it going?"

"This is only my second day, but okay, so far. I'm practicing those mind tricks. They help with the sore muscles. I won't screw up this time."

"I have faith in you."

JR's chest expanded. "Chelsea and I opened a bank account to put away money for our own place."

He seemed to be growing up at last. Jillian must be relieved. "Good man. Did you think any more about your GED?"

"I called about it after work yesterday. There's a class this summer I'll probably sign up for."

"Smart thinking." Rafe clapped his shoulder. "Is your sister ready for the art festival this weekend?"

"Finally. Miller and Chelsea are helping her load Miller's truck right now."

"Two days early?"

"You wouldn't believe all the stuff she's bringing. It'll take hours to pack everything into the truck. She wants to go tomorrow so she and Chelsea can get the booth set up and open with a bang on Friday. Miller offered to sleep over. That way, they can leave first thing in the morning. Chelsea will follow them in Jill's car."

Stuck on the fact Miller would spend the night, Rafe paid no attention to the rest. "With you and Chelsea in the spare bedroom, where will Miller sleep?"

"Beats me. I don't pry into my sister's private life."

According to JR, Jillian and Miller were friends. Now Rafe wondered whether their friendship included benefits.

The thought of her in bed with another man was too much. He let out an unhappy growl.

JR's eyes widened. "Chill, Rafe. As I said before, Jill and Miller aren't into each other that way. The living room couch unfolds into a bed. He'll probably bunk there."

Rafe could live with that.

"I don't know why you care," JR went on. "You say you aren't into her."

Rafe wasn't supposed to be, not anymore.

JR's eyes narrowed. "You *are*."

"Don't you have work to do?"

Despite Rafe's scowl, the smart aleck had the gall to grin. "Later."

In a foul mood, Rafe stalked around, waiting for Tim. When the builder showed up some quarter of an hour later, Rafe spent all of two minutes talking to him before he grew antsy and left.

He knew exactly what he ought to do—forget Jillian and move on. But how in hell did he do that?

17

Around noon Thursday, Jillian, Chelsea, and Miller transferred the last of the crates from Miller's truck to the booth where Jillian and Chelsea would spend their waking hours for the next three days.

Over a hundred artists and craftspeople milled around the fairgrounds, chatting with each other and working to create tempting and welcoming spaces for tomorrow's opening day. Jillian and Miller greeted old friends and made new ones. Chelsea fit in well and seemed to enjoy meeting everyone.

Forty-something Miller, tall, with thinning hair and smile creases around his eyes, checked his watch. "I'd best get back to Guff's Lake. I promised my assistant manager some of the afternoon off."

"It's lunchtime. Let me buy you a sandwich first," Jillian offered. Nearby, an enterprising restaurant had set up a food stand for hungry artists.

Miller shook his head. "You sprang for dinner last night, fed me this morning, and filled my truck's gas tank. That's enough. I'll grab something on the way out of town."

"Okay. Thanks for lugging everything down here and helping us unload it. I owe you."

"Just keep sending those pottery students my way for their supplies." Miller kissed her cheek. "May you sell out and come home with a bunch of new orders."

Jillian held up her crossed fingers.

"You've been talking about and working on product for this festival since I first met you," Chelsea commented as Miller strode toward the parking lot and disappeared. "Now it's finally here... I guess I thought you'd be more jazzed."

Lately, working up enthusiasm for anything wasn't easy. Determined to shake off the blues, Jillian forced a smile. "I'm super excited. It's going to be a great festival."

Running the booth would keep her too busy to even think about Rafe. "I am running low," she added. "I need food, and I'll bet you do, too. Let's get sandwiches. We'll eat, then organize the merchandise, lock up, and check into the motel."

Taking a break from fence building in the late afternoon, Rafe and Adam reached into the cooler for a couple of beers and settled into lawn chairs on Adam's backyard patio. Overhead, chattering birds flew back and forth, building nests, and a couple of squirrels chased each other up a tree.

Adam popped off the screw-top, tilted the bottle

Rafe's way in a silent salute, and drank. "That art festival in Medford is this weekend. You could drive over there and talk to her."

No need to say her name. They both knew who he meant. "What for?" Rafe said.

"Because you've barely cracked a grin in weeks, and I'm tired of looking at your gloomy mug."

"Lay it on me, why don't you." Rafe sipped his own beer. "There's nothing for Jillian and me to discuss because there's nothing between us. Not anymore."

His bud snorted. "Get real, man. This thing between you two is unlike any of your past relationships. It's serious."

No point in denying that. Rafe blew out a heavy breath. "I can't give her what she wants."

"So you keep repeating. If you remember, I used to sing the same song—until I woke up and realized I wanted to be with Sam forever."

"Your issues are totally different from mine."

"True, but I have some doozies, stuff I'm still wrestling with."

They both went quiet for a while, sipping beer and enjoying the afternoon sun, before Adam swiveled his head Rafe's way.

"Answer me straight from the gut—do you trust Jillian?"

"I would trust her with my life," Rafe replied without hesitation.

Had he actually said that? While he was still reeling from the realization, Adam gave a sage nod.

"Maybe it's time you took deeper look at yourself and what you want."

18

Outside Rafe's place, all was dark and silent. Not even the first birds stirring—too damn early to get up, especially on a Friday.

He'd never considered himself a deep thinker, especially about his own stuff, and after a restless night spent turning Adam's unasked-for advice around in his mind, he had yet to figure out a damn thing. Or sleep.

Giving up on both, he left his bed. Bleary-eyed and sorely in need of caffeine, he padded downstairs. He let Calvin into the back yard, started a pot of coffee, dumped a can of dog food into Calvin's bowl, and let him back in.

The Vizsla wolfed down his meal—then licked his lips and looked to Rafe with a what's next expression.

"Give me a break," Rafe muttered.

It'd be several hours before the morning paper arrived, but no big—at the moment, he had zero interest in reading. Too unsettled to sit and wait for the coffeemaker to do its thing, he prowled around the main floor, Calvin obediently at his side.

"It's this thing with Jillian," he explained, questioning his sanity for sharing his problems with his dog. But with his ears cocked forward, the animal appeared to be listening. "For the life of me, I can't let go of her and move on. I'm driving myself crazy."

The coffeemaker finally gurgled to a stop. Rafe filled a mug and set it on the breakfast bar. Suddenly hungry, he grabbed a bowl, a box of cereal, and a half-gallon of milk from the fridge. Moments later, he plunked onto a barstool and dug in.

Two cups of coffee and three bowls of cereal later, he'd filled his belly. Oddly, he still felt empty.

Wearing an expectant expression, Calvin sat on his haunches at Rafe's feet, silently inviting him to say more.

Rafe rubbed his chest. "There's a hole in here, and I don't know how to fill it."

His steadfast pal did his version of a canine eye roll and tossed his head.

"You think I'm in love with Jillian." Rafe scoffed. "You're as bad as Adam. You both know me better than that. I don't do love."

The dog scrambled up, trotted toward the back door where his leash hung on a hook, and barked at it.

Rafe frowned. "Nope, we're not going to her place to talk. She isn't there. She's at the art festival in Medford."

Stubborn gaze still pinned on the leash, Calvin let out a soft whine.

"If you think I'm going to drive ninety miles one

way for a conversation, think again. Anyway, she'll be way too busy for us."

Yet despite the objections Rafe voiced, he seriously considered making the drive. Which showed how off his game he was.

Serious—that was how Adam had labeled the Jillian situation. Rafe had to agree, even if he didn't want to feel so strongly about anyone and had never expected to.

As for the trust thing he'd blurted out on the patio... Still shaking his head, he slid off the stool, loaded his dishes into the dishwasher, and put away the cereal and milk.

He wanted to keep seeing Jillian, but she wouldn't allow him back into her life unless he bought into her dream—a ring on her finger and the whole nine yards that came with it. Commitment and marriage and kids.

"Except for Grandma Donato and a couple of teachers, I didn't think I would ever trust a woman," he confessed to Calvin. "But Jillian... There's nothing flaky about her. She's loyal to her brother. No matter what, she has his back. If I let her, she'd have mine, too. Kind of like my crewmates at the fire department."

Only different. Warmer and a whole lot sweeter. "She's always been straight with me, sharing her thoughts and feelings, regardless of the consequences," he went on. "She's amazing, all right—one in a million."

Calvin nodded.

But could Rafe make the kind of commitment Jillian deserved? Having never pictured himself as a husband or a father, he found the idea intimidating.

Yet, here he was, considering it. Spooked, he shoved his hands into his pockets, glanced unseeing at the kitchen floor, and then began to pace the room.

Damn, he was confused...

His cursed dog bumped against his leg and stared up at him. "I'm no coward, so quit giving me that look," Rafe warned in his sternest tone.

Calvin appeared unruffled, his gaze never wavering.

"I've had it with you and your accusations," Rafe grumbled. "You're going outside again, and I'm heading upstairs to shower, shave, and get dressed. And, yeah, figure out what I want."

ALL THAT THINKING led to Rafe showing up at the Medford Fairgrounds some hours later. He still wasn't sure why he'd come or exactly what he wanted, only that he needed to see Jillian and talk with her. He'd figure out what to say then.

With live music, mouthwatering aromas filling the air from the food booths and tons of people with money to spend, the art festival was in full swing. Pulling Calvin to a stop, he studied the map provided when he'd paid his admission fee. Jillian's booth was smack in the middle of the action—the ideal place to draw in lots of customers.

Between the milling crowds and the distractions pulling Calvin in the wrong direction, it took a while for Rafe to reach her booth. Some half a dozen people looked over her pieces, with five more lined up to pay for purchases. Wearing a wide grin, Chelsea handed a young couple a carefully wrapped parcel and receipt. At the opposite end of the counter, Jillian engaged in conversation with two middle-aged women.

Taking advantage of the moment, he drank in the sight of her. Tall and lovely, her face animated and alive. So beautiful, this woman he loved.

Love. The word clicked into his mind and settled in, as if it belonged there, and suddenly, everything felt right.

With absolute, deep-in-his-soul clarity, Rafe knew he loved Jillian and understood that he always would. Awed, he shook his head.

At last, if sensing his gaze, she looked straight at him. Startled, confused.

His.

And just like that, his formerly empty chest expanded, growing full to bursting. The slow, goofy grin he'd scorned Adam for bloomed on his own face.

"Excuse me," he said, pushing through the line. He hopped over the counter—not so easy, but with years of firefighting training behind him, doable.

Her eyebrows jumped comically up her forehead. "What are you doing here?"

"I need to have a word with you—privately. Chelsea, will you take over and watch Calvin?"

All eyes, the girl nodded. "Sure, Rafe."

Jillian dug in her heels. "I'm kind of busy here." She gestured at the waiting crowd. "Can this wait?"

"Nope."

She clamped her lips together, showing him what she thought of his reply. "It'll have to. Just now, I'm not going anyplace."

"You want me to do this here?"

"How am I supposed to answer that, when I have no idea why you're crowding Chelsea and me in our booth?"

"Fine. We'll do it here. I miss you."

"You drove ninety miles to say that?" Jillian crossed her arms and eyed him. "Your timing is a little off."

Yeah, *I miss you* did sound lame. "Sometimes it takes a while for me to get things through this thick skull of mine. But when I do..." Rafe rubbed the back of his neck. "The thing is..."

The area had grown quiet, nearby shoppers all eyes, waiting for what happened next. As if he and Jillian were starring in some spectator sport. Not exactly optimal, but now that he knew what he wanted, he wouldn't let a bunch of nosy people get in his way.

"I've been thinking a lot about us," he said. "And I realize I..." He had to stop and swallow past the lump in his throat. "I love you."

Jillian's jaw dropped. "But you don't fall in love."

"Apparently I do."

"Are you sure?"

"More than I've ever been about anything."

The stunned look on her face was priceless. And a little off-putting. The feelings she had for him must not be as strong as he'd figured. "You're not happy about this," he said, crestfallen.

"You have that all wrong. But why couldn't you have waited to tell me until after the festival?"

Rafe didn't understand. "I don't follow."

"Then I could show you in private exactly how I feel. Because I love you, too."

She loved him.

He teared up and quickly swiped his eyes. "Then you'll be my girl? There's a future in it for you. For us."

When they were home again, he would take her out to Guff's Lake and kiss her under the ash tree. Sealing their life together.

"I'll be your girl and then some." Jillian twined her arms around his neck.

Holding back none of the warmth crowding his chest, he kissed her. When he let her go, she wore the dreamy look he'd come to expect. To adore.

Everyone applauded.

"You should get back to work," he said gruffly.

"Back?" She looked confused.

"To all these patient customers."

"Right. Where can I find you later?"

"I'll let you know as soon as I get a room for you, me, and Calvin. You don't mind staying in your own room, do you, Chelsea?"

The girl's smile filled her face. "Not at all."

"You'll never find a room," Jillian said. "With the festival, all the hotels and motels are booked up."

"I know most of the firefighters in Rogue Valley. Let me make some calls. Bye, babe."

"Bye." A love-filled smile lit her face. "I love you, Rafe."

"Back at ya."

He gave the gawkers a thumbs-up and stepped into the brilliant day.

THE END

THANK you for letting me share my stories with you! There are 12 sexy firefighter books planned for the **Heroes of Rogue Valley: Calendar Guys**

IF YOU ENJOYED **MR. FEBRUARY**, help others find this book by recommending it to your friends and by writing a review. If you would like to know when my next release is available and other fun stuff, sign up for my newsletter here: www.annroth.net

VISIT ME AT FACEBOOK FACEBOOK.COM/ANNROTHAUTHORPAGE
Follow me on Twitter @Ann_Roth
Email me at ann@annroth.net
Visit my website www.annroth.net

THANKS, and until next time,
Ann

PLEASE ENJOY this excerpt from **Mr. March:**

Firefighter Gus Viggio needs to convince the stubborn great aunt who raised him and recently suffered a stroke to give up the house that has become too much for her. When she refuses, Gus enlists help from her flamboyant hairstylist, Wanda Lippman. The two women get along well, and Gus's great aunt just might listen to her. Wanda and Gus have each been hurt by love, and neither is ready to venture back into those dangerous waters anytime soon. But sometimes the heart knows best...

The second Gus Viggio offered his great aunt Polly a boost into his Jeep Cherokee, she shook her cane and fixed him with that stubborn *I'm not a helpless old lady yet* look that warned him to back off. God help him if he attempted to buckle her in.

Hands shoved into his jeans pockets, he stood by the open passenger door. Just in case. She wasn't as strong as she used to be, and those arthritic hands made even fastening the seatbelt difficult.

While he waited, he squinted against the sun, bright but not strong enough to take the chill out of the April morning. Almost overnight, spring had sprung in the Rogue Valley. Here in Guff's Lake, grass, shrubs and flowers, dormant through the winter, had made up for lost time and grown by leaps and bounds.

"My yard is mess," Aunt Polly lamented.

Once an avid gardener, she could no longer handle yard work. Gus had taken over the job, with occasional help from his father. "Dad and I will stop by and take care of it this weekend."

Maintaining the large front and back yards took a big chunk of time, but Gus didn't mind. He loved Aunt Polly dearly. When his mom had left, his great aunt had invited him and his dad to move in and had raised Gus as her own.

Years ago, they'd decided to dispense with the "great" label, respectively shortening their names to "Aunt Polly" and "nephew." Not that "aunt" cut it, either. She was more a mother and grandmother rolled into one. He would do anything for her. Anything.

Buckled in at last, Aunt Polly folded her hands in her lap. "What are we waiting for?" she said with an impish look. "Let's boogie."

He grinned at her word choice. "You're in a good mood today."

"On such a beautiful morning, how could I not be?" She slipped a pair of sunglasses over her bifocals. "Besides, it isn't every day my favorite nephew and two of his fellow firefighters take me to lunch at Ellen's."

The stuffy restaurant wasn't at the top of Gus's go-to list, but his aunt loved eating there, and his buds enjoyed her company, so they tolerated the place.

"Your *only* nephew," he reminded her, pulling on his Ray-Bans.

"If I had a dozen, you'd still be my favorite."

"Not favorite enough to take my advice."

Her lips thinned. "Don't you dare start in on me about my living arrangements, Augusto Frances Viggio. I'm perfectly able to take care of myself, and you know it."

The use of Gus's full name meant she was seriously irritated, but didn't change the fact he disagreed with her.

Insisting on independence, she lived alone in her big, old house. No amount of reasoning or cajoling had convinced her to downsize and move into an apartment in a retirement community.

She did allow him to chauffeur her around, thanks to a stroke ten months ago that had put an end to her driving. Gus didn't mind shuttling her where she needed to go—when he could. Between him and his dad, they managed.

"If and when I decide to leave, I promise to let you know," she added. "But don't hold your breath." Raising her chin, she changed the subject. "As I was saying, you are my favorite nephew. Who else can I rely on to take me to my weekly hair appointment with Wanda?"

Gus tabled the conversation about moving—for the moment. "No problem."

Tommie's Hair and Nails was an easy ten-minute drive from Aunt Polly's house. "I need to schedule an inspection at Tommie's. May as well set that up today."

"For the safety project?"

"That's the one."

Gus had been tasked with checking fire and smoke alarms in every commercial and multi-dwelling residential structure as well as updating computer diagrams with the safest routes into and out of each. Important information that was posted in every building for both civilians and emergency responders to use during emergencies.

Gathering and collating all that data in the town of almost twenty-thousand people was taking more time than Gus had estimated. When he'd started ten weeks earlier, he'd promised the captain a finish date of early August. As tight as the deadline now seemed, he intended to deliver, even if it meant working off the clock.

No longer cross with him, Aunt Polly tilted her lips into a fond smile. "Not just anyone is strong and smart enough to be a firefighter. I'm so proud of you."

Gus's chest expanded. Not one for big displays of emotion, he gave a modest shrug.

"I can't wait to tell Wanda about lunch today," Aunt Polly said. "She'll be all ears. She's a darling, that one."

Darling wasn't the word that came to mind when Gus thought of Wanda Lipmann, who looked to be in her late twenties. He never knew what to expect when he saw her. Short and curvy, she wore her clothes bright and tight, and she changed her hair-style and color a couple times a month. Talk about unsettling.

They hadn't spoken much, except to say hi and bye when he brought Aunt Polly in and picked her up.

His aunt cast him a sly look. "If you'd get to know Wanda, you'd realize how special she is."

Gus rolled his eyes. "Stop right there. You are not fixing me up—now or ever."

"But it's been almost a year since your breakup with Delores."

"Denise," he corrected. "I'm way over her."

For sure. After she'd pressured him one too many times to get married, he'd decided to break up with her. Then Aunt Polly had had her stroke. "Trust me, if I had time, I'd be dating. I happen to have a lot on my plate."

Between working at the Guff's Lake Fire Department, looking after Aunt Polly, and running his one-man classic car restoration business, Gus was overbooked.

Not that he wanted to give up any of his responsibilities. His car business relaxed him and felt more like play. Currently, he was restoring a 1965 classic Lincoln. His customer had agreed to pay top dollar, with a bonus if he finished in time for the classic car show in mid-May.

Whipping off her sunglasses, Aunt Polly gave him the no-nonsense look that had always worked during her librarian days, her still-bright eyes serious behind the bifocals. "At thirty-two, you're not getting any younger."

"Don't hold back."

"Have I ever? It's time you found a wife and settled down. That should be your priority, but because it isn't, you need help. Mine."

She'd been after him to get married since the day he turned thirty, nagging him with a dogged determination that wouldn't quit.

Gus narrowed his eyes a fraction. "Stop."

"I will not." She sniffed. "Come October, I'll be eighty. I've earned the right to speak my mind."

"Like that's anything new. You know I'm not against marriage, but there's no guarantee it'll happen."

"Pish posh," Aunt Polly said. "Of course it will."

His parents had split up when he was seven, but he had good little-kid memories. Settling down and having two or three children appealed to him. But to date, every one of his serious relationships had gone south.

In matters of the heart, he'd begun to think he was just like his father. This apple hadn't fallen far from the tree.

Gus pulled onto Brewster Street, home to a dozen small businesses on the west side of town. Tommie's Hair and Nails salon was always buzzing, mostly with women, and judging by the number of cars parked in the salon lot, this morning was no different.

"This is a wash-and-trim appointment. I'll be done in about thirty minutes," his aunt said as opened the passenger door for her. "Since you need to schedule that inspection, you may as well wait inside."

Having just come off forty-eight hours—two back-to-back shifts—at the Guff's Lake Fire Department, with a couple calls in the dead of night, Gus planned to grab some quick Z's in the Jeep while Aunt Polly had her hair done. He'd deliver her to Wanda, schedule the inspection, then make a bee-line for the Jeep.

Refusing his arm, she relied on her cane. In the sunlight, the sparkly *Tommie's Hair and Nails* sign on the door glittered. Gus ushered his aunt inside and removed his shades.

The half-dozen or so females in the process of

manicures and haircuts stopped chattering and stared at him.

Every week he brought Aunt Polly here, but you'd think they'd never seen him in the salon. Maybe it was his size. Bigger than many men, he'd grown used to curious looks. Lately, more than usual, thanks to the firefighter calendar.

Feeling awkward, he nodded at Carol Sue, who had about ten years on him.

"Nice to see you, Polly. Hi there, Gus," she said, batting her lashes at him.

"Hey," he replied, courteous but not too friendly.

A flirt and a gossip, Carol Sue lived to spread rumors. Here in Guff's Lake, information spread faster than a forest fire in summer. Gus preferred to stay out of her stories.

"Who do I talk to about scheduling a salon inspection?" he asked.

"That would be either Tommie or Wanda. Tommie's out just now, but Wanda is here. I'll let her know you and Polly have arrived. Help yourselves to coffee. The one with the orange band is the decaf you want, Polly. The other is leaded. Enjoy." She sashayed off.

Gus got Aunt Polly settled on the sofa and brought her a decaf with sugar and creamer. He filled a Styrofoam cup with the leaded stuff and sat in a chair. A few sips in, the "Employees Only" door at the rear of the salon opened. Wanda and two stylists stepped inside.

Sticking close to the door, all three glanced his way and whispered. God knew what they were saying. As long as it didn't go on too long, Gus didn't care.

He took another few sips of coffee before Wanda started forward.

POLLY BECKER RANKED among Wanda's favorite customers. She wasn't so comfortable with Polly's great nephew.

At six foot four and two hundred thirty pounds —details everyone who owned a Guff's Lake Fire Department calendar knew—Gus, aka Mr. March, was a strikingly handsome man. All solid muscle, he was built more like a super-fit linebacker than a firefighter. The piercing green eyes and short, light-brown hair with a hint of red didn't hurt, either. Looking at him, a woman would have to be dead not to have heart palpitations.

The calendar, sold to raise money for the station's benefit fund, had turned Gus and the eleven men featured into local celebrities.

Nadia, a stylist and close friend Wanda had been chatting with in back, elbowed her. "He always drops Polly off and leaves," she said in a low voice. "Carol Sue says he wants to talk to you today. I wonder why?"

"What does it matter, as long as I'm in the same room as him?" murmured Rochelle, Wanda's second closest friend. She worked from noon to closing on Wednesdays, but had come in early to accommodate a customer. She fanned herself. "He's even more gorgeous in person."

In place of his usual T-shirt, jeans and weathered leather jacket, he'd switched it up in a pressed blue shirt, dark pants and polished black oxfords. He looked good in dress clothes, but he looked equally fine in casuals.

"Maybe I'll move my schedule around and start working early on Wednesdays." Rochelle gave Wanda a sideways glance. "Unless you have dibs on him?"

Currently, both Rochelle and Nadia were single and in the market for a boyfriend. Wanda frowned. "Tommie depends on you to work late Tuesdays and Wednesdays. And don't forget, I'm taking a break from men."

Her friends shared a look. "You say that every time you go through a breakup," Nadia pointed out. "Until some cute guy asks you out. Then you're off and running again."

"After I've turned down every guy who asked me out the past six-and-a-half months? If that isn't serious, I don't know what is."

She refused to date until she figured out how to win and hold a man's love with more than good sex. She had the sex part down but not the rest, and her heart had been broken more times than she could count.

The latest split with Larry had hurt almost as much as losing Wayne ten years earlier. In hindsight, she realized much of the pain stemmed from her seriously wounded pride. She'd tried her best to keep Larry interested but had failed. Yet again. She didn't think she could survive one more breakup.

"To clarify," Rochelle said, "you're not interested in Gus Viggio."

"Right."

Even if a mere glance at the man caused a spike in her pulse rate, he'd never given her more than a brief greeting and a cursory glance. A good thing, too. Otherwise, she might be tempted to forget she'd sworn off guys, proving her friends right.

"Polly's waiting for me," she said. "And apparently so is Gus."

Curious as she was about what he could possibly want, she paused and fluffed her layered, purple-streaked, blond hair—a far cry from its dull-brown natural color. She strutted forward, her teal, three-inch ankle boots clicking smartly across the tile floor. The walk had taken years to perfect.

As she drew closer, Gus pushed to his feet. His great aunt had raised him right.

"Morning, Polly," Wanda said, with a warm smile.

The older woman beamed. "I like your hair, Wanda. Those purple streaks are fun. And what a snazzy outfit."

"Thanks." Wanda smoothed her short-sleeve, lavender tee over her hips. Even with the three extra inches of the ankle boots, she was only five feet six. She tilted her head back a little to greet the firefighter. "Hello, Gus."

He nodded, his expression impossible to read, and gave her a once-over from her head to the hint of cleavage, courtesy of the low scoop neck, where his gaze lingered a beat longer than an uninterested man's should have. Then past her flared, teal skirt to her black leggings.

Pride surged through her. As with her walk, the cutting-edge hairstyles and clothing had never been natural to her. Neither was being bubbly and talkative. But wanting to be noticed and liked by men, even though she'd temporarily sworn off them, she'd adjusted. Her efforts had paid off. Getting a date when she wanted one was never a problem, and both male and female customers kept coming back.

Proving Cindy right, for once.

"I'm told you're the one to see about scheduling a safety inspection," he said, his deep, sexy voice vibrating through her.

Safety inspection—of course. A little part of her had assumed he wanted information of the personal kind. What a relief he didn't. Or so she assured herself. Yet something inside her deflated a fraction. "I'm the one, all right."

"Do you have any time Monday?"

"We're closed that day, but I guess that'd work."

"If you're closed, who'll let me in?"

"Either Tommie or me."

Likely Wanda. Tommie had just turned sixty-five and decided to retire at the end of September. Wanda wanted to buy the business and the building—provided she saved up enough for the down-payment necessary to secure a loan. Although she still needed a fair chunk of change, she'd assured Tommie that when the time came, she would have the required funds.

The past few months, Tommie had been

teaching her the ins and outs of running the salon, and slowly giving Wanda more responsibility.

"Your aunt should be ready to go in about a half hour," she told Gus. "You can pick her up then."

"He's going to wait here today." Polly showered him with a fond grin. "Then he's taking me to lunch at Ellen's."

No wonder he'd dressed up. "Lucky you." Wanda sighed.

She'd always wanted to try the upscale restaurant, but not one of her boyfriends had ever taken her there. "Have a seat in the waiting area, Gus. I'll bring her to you when we finish. Come on, Polly, let's make you gorgeous."

She offered her arm, but Polly rebuffed her. Thanks to her shoes, Wanda stood some two inches over the woman. She also moved a lot quicker. She slowed way down, and they made their way to her station across the way.

Or tried.

Polly dug in her heels and waved her cane at Gus. "Aren't you coming with us?"

"My station is small, and there's no place for you to sit," Wanda pointed out. "You'll be more comfortable in the waiting area."

So would she. If he hovered around, she wouldn't be able to relax.

"Nonsense. He'll bring a seat with him," Polly insisted. "I want him to see what you do."

"Aunt Polly..."

Wanda didn't understand Gus's warning look."

Lips compressed, Polly turned away from his gaze.

While he returned to the waiting area to grab a chair, Wanda helped her into the salon chair. She fastened a large plastic smock around Polly's neck, gently tipped her back to wash her hair, and wondered what her customer was up to.

Coming soon! **Mr. April:**

When firefighter Owen Ayers agrees to let freelance writer Hallie Sawyer shadow him to gather information for her article about Guff's Lake Fire Department, he assumes the task will be easy. Instead, sharing his time with the plucky brunette proves challenging—and not just on a professional level. Burned by a failed marriage and wary of getting involved, Owen is irresistibly drawn to Hallie. After suffering through the unimaginable pain of losing her fiancé and unborn daughter, Hallie is determined to rebuild her life by avoiding relationships and focusing on her career. But sexy Owen threatens to breach her protective shell. The healing power of love just might save them both.

Please enjoy this excerpt from **Mr. January:**

Senior Firefighter Adam Healey is a man with a mission: get promoted to lieutenant at the Guff's Lake Fire Department. It's time, but more important, the promotion will finally earn him the respect of his dying father. Single mom Samantha Everett's deadbeat ex has left her to fend for herself, and she's working hard to support her young son with her baking business. Neither

Adam nor Samantha is looking for a relationship. But love has a way of surprising people...

AT THE UNGODLY hour of five-forty-five a.m., Samantha Everett pulled into the delivery slot at Rosemary's Breakfast Nook. In the dark, the twin beams of the hatchback's headlights spotlighted the swirling snow. Well, it was early January in Rogue Valley.

"Please don't stick," she muttered under her breath, dreading the thought of putting on the tire chains.

Although so far, she hadn't needed them. When she'd moved to Guff's Lake six months earlier, locals had assured her that the usual winter temperatures tended to hover above freezing.

So different from the bone-chilling cold and frequent snowstorms in Enterprise.

"Look, Mom! Snow!" William chimed from the backseat.

At the age of five, he was delighted by almost everything—even at this hour. His joy was contagious, and Samantha's irritation dissipated like smoke. "I see it."

"Let me out." He unbuckled his car seat straps and bounced in anticipation for her to open the door.

Yawning—thanks to only five hours' sleep— Samantha exited the car. The building's perimeter lights cast long shadows across the nearly vacant concrete lot, a large area shared by several businesses. The few cars here now belonged to Rosemary, the cook, and wait staff. Rosemary's Breakfast Nook served the best breakfast in town, and snow or none, when the café opened at six, business would be brisk.

Despite the relative stillness, it was best to be safe. "Hold onto my coat," she directed.

Her itching-to-be-independent son grumbled but obeyed. Samantha opened the hatchback and jockeyed a dolly cart to the pavement. William helped her unfold it. Then she carefully loaded it with today's order—eight dozen still-warm cinnamon rolls, and six dozen each assorted muffins and scones. Her biggest order to date would net her more money than she'd ever earned as a baker in Enterprise.

Rosemary wouldn't pay her until a week from Friday, but Samantha had already divided and earmarked every penny. Groceries and other household expenses, bakery supplies, and the savings account for attorney fees.

To date, Jeff had ignored every one of the financial and custodial obligations spelled out in the divorce decree. Not one penny of child support or money for the debts he'd saddled her with, and not one request to see his son. Good riddance!

After all this time, Samantha doubted she'd ever hear from Jeff. She didn't need an attorney right now, but Betty Randall, her grandmotherly neighbor, believed that she did. Just in case. The woman had been so insistent Samantha had lost sleep over it. Mainly because Betty gave sound advice, unlike the unsolicited guidance from Samantha's parents.

William helped push the dolly toward the delivery entrance. As always, the door was unlocked for her, and easy to shoulder open and back through. Pausing inside the door, she brushed the snow off her son's parka and hat and then took care of her own coat.

The warmth, the fragrant aroma of freshly brewing coffee, and the haze from the sizzling vat of oil greeted her. A fragrant, smoky scent filled the air, and Samantha's mouth watered.

"Good morning," she greeted Rosemary and her longtime boyfriend and cook, José.

Round and perpetually cheerful, the forty-something restaurant owner greeted Samantha and William with her usual toothy smile. "Good morning." She winked at William. "How are you, sunshine?"

His small brow furrowed. "My name is William Tyler Everett Jones." Samantha had changed her last name back to Everett but had left her son's name intact.

From the time he'd first formed sentences, he'd insisted that everyone use his given name.

"I know that, darlin', but seeing you always makes me smile, and a true smile is as warm as the sunshine," Rosemary said. "Do you two have time for breakfast this morning?"

"Say yes, Mom." William gave Samantha the round-eyed, pleading look she'd never been able to resist.

Guff's Lake Bed & Breakfast, her only other paying client so far, didn't expect her until seven, and William's half-day kindergarten wouldn't start for several hours yet. She ought to use the time on housework—keeping the kitchen spotless was a constant chore.

But she really could use another cup of coffee and something to eat besides the bowl of cold cereal waiting for her at home.

"We'd love to have breakfast here," she said. "Can I put in an order for José's hash browns?"

José chuckled. "You bet. Bacon and eggs, too?"

"Yes, please."

"And cocoa?" William asked, going all round-eyed again.

Rosemary nodded. "I'll bring it with your breakfast."

As she filled a coffee mug for Samantha, Jana, one of the waitresses and Samantha's best friend, entered the kitchen through the restaurant's swinging doors.

"I thought I heard you in here. Can you believe it's snowing? I'll bet you love that, William. Let's get the case loaded."

Samantha wheeled the dolly to the counter out front, where bright walls and colorful posters added a homey, cheerful feel to the restaurant. She and William kept Jana company while she arranged Samantha's baked goods in the case and placed the printed "Treats by Samantha" sign in plain view. What didn't fit stayed in the delivery boxes for restocking the case until the restaurant closed at one.

Rosemary inspected the finished display with a satisfied nod. "You and William go on and make yourselves at home," she told Samantha. "I'll bring your food out shortly."

Samantha let her son choose where to sit. He led her to his favorite spot, a booth in front of the big picture window that faced the door. With the restaurant minutes from opening, Jana and the three other servers bustled around, seeing to last-minute details. Then one of the waitresses unlocked the door and welcomed in the morning's first customers.

Moments later, Rosemary delivered breakfast to Samantha and William. While Samantha enjoyed her food and coffee, her son chattered nonstop. During recess at Guff's Lake Elementary, the school he proudly called his own, he would have a snowball fight and build a snowman with Douglas and Harper, his two best friends.

Customers steadily streamed in to eat at the restaurant or collect their breakfast and morning coffee to go, some alone, others in groups. The almost twenty thousand Guff's Lake residents tended to be a friendly bunch, and even the people Samantha didn't recognize greeted her with nods and smiles.

Sipping a second cup of coffee and staring out the window with relief as the snow let up, she watched an orange 4Runner pull into the lot. A solid-looking male slid out of the driver's seat. Dressed in a leather bomber jacket, jeans, and a baseball cap, he wore a cast on one foot and a sling on his arm. A backpack swung from the other shoulder. Even with his arm injury and hobbling gait, he managed to move with a purposeful stride that for some reason reminded her of a big, sleek jungle cat. A tiger or a puma came to mind.

The sky had lightened a fraction, and between the approaching dawn and the perimeter lights, she easily made out his face.

And oh, what a face! The broad forehead, strong chin, and straight nose only added to his overall attractiveness. With a jolt of awareness, she recognized him. Adam Healey, aka Mr. January in the Guff's Lake Fire Department calendar that had come out last month, just in time for Christmas, as part of an ongoing fund-raising drive for the fire department's benefit fund.

The calendar featured twelve of the most gorgeous men Samantha had ever laid eyes on, and listed fascinating information, including height, weight, and marital status. She recalled that Adam was single.

Every female in town, along with a host of men and all the local businesses, had purchased calendars. At Rosemary's Breakfast Nook, the calendar hung prominently in the display case, with Adam in his firefighter hat, grinning and shirtless under a deep blue sky. In the background, the snowy Siskiyou Mountains. Samantha glanced at it and blew out an admiring sigh.

Everyone knew that the guys from the Guff's Lake Fire Department hung out here, since the station a was mere two blocks away. Ordinarily Samantha came and went before any of them wandered in for coffee and breakfast. But today...

Adam must have sensed her staring at him, for his gaze met hers through the window. Embarrassed, she turned her attention to William.

"—read more *Charlotte's Web* to us today," he said, still chattering about his kindergarten class.

"That's such a great book," she replied.

The door opened, and a gust of cold air rushed in. But the man who shut it behind him sucked the chill right out of the room.

Adam's eyes were still riveted on her. She couldn't seem to tear her glance away, either. Up this close, his pale-blue eyes were even more striking than they were in the calendar photo. The color of the sky just before the sun rose.

It had been a while since a man turned her head, and she wasn't sure she liked that fluttery feeling of attraction. She'd moved here to escape Enterprise and the past and start fresh, and for the first time in more than three years, she was happy. Between taking care of William and supporting the two of them with her baked-goods business, socializing with friends and a weekly knitting class, she had filled her life to the brim. She didn't have time to look at a man, let alone date.

Or so she assured herself.

Ready to leave, she pushed to her feet and stacked her breakfast dishes to make cleanup easier for Jana. Her friend sashayed toward Adam with her hips swaying and a longing look on her face.

Jana was dating someone, but she wasn't blind. By the similar expressions the other waitresses wore, they were just as smitten. So were the other women in the café, who checked Adam out with approval.

"Hey there, Adam," Jana said with a flirty smile.

"I didn't expect to see you this early in the morning. How are that wrist and ankle?"

"Getting better every day."

"Adam!" Rosemary bustled over with a grin on her face. "You're just in time to meet Samantha Everett, the bakery goddess behind Samantha's Treats, the goodies that bring you back every morning. Adam's a huge fan," she told Samantha.

"That's right. Hey." He touched the bill of his hat.

He was a big man, a good six inches taller than Samantha and powerfully built. Even wearing ankle boots that added two inches to her five-feet-six-inch height, she felt small.

"Hi," she answered, cupping her empty mug to her chest. As if it could deflect the mesmerizing warmth in his eyes.

"William, this is Adam Healey," Rosemary continued. "He's a firefighter."

"For real?" Her son looked starstruck.

"How you doing, sport?" Adam asked.

"My name is William Tyler Everett Jones."

"That's quite a mouthful. Mind if I call you sport?"

"Okay."

This was a first, and surprised Samantha.

Adam sniffed. "I smell smoke."

Right then, a waitress hurried out of the kitchen balancing several plates. Wisps of smoke followed her. The smoke alarm screeched, and people stopped eating.

"Everyone, clear out," Adam ordered in a booming voice. "Keep an eye on this." He handed his backpack to Samantha. On his way to the kitchen he pulled his arm from the sling, whipped out his phone and made a call.

"What's that noise? Where is he going, Mom?" William asked as he and Samantha donned their coats and headed toward the door.

"To see what set off the smoke detector."

"Why can't we go with him?"

"We don't want to get in the way. Besides, we need to get going." But she had Adam's backpack and she'd left her dolly behind the display case.

She would have handed the backpack to someone and come back later for the dolly, but her son dug in his heels. "I want to wait and see what happens," he said, his breath clouding in the cold.

The stubborn set of his jaw reminded her of Jeff when they were still married. Before he'd walked away from her and William, just days before her twenty-seventh birthday. The last time William had seen his father, he'd been all of twenty-six months old. Yet somehow, he'd picked up that stubborn look.

Getting him into the car without a battle wouldn't be easy, and Samantha didn't have the energy for an argument. With a sigh, she nodded and waited out front with the other restaurant patrons.

❧

A BURNER HAD CAUGHT FIRE, and thick smoke rapidly filled the kitchen. Adam grabbed the fire extinguisher and went to work. In seconds, he had the flames out.

"Open the back door and get some fresh air in here," he directed.

Rosemary complied, and José swiped his brow. "That was close. I shouldn't have set that towel so close to the flames. It won't happen again."

Adam nodded. "Hang on while I call the station." He made the call then disconnected. "They're coming anyway. It's what we do."

His sprained wrist hurt like hell. Should've been more careful when he'd hefted the extinguisher. But his focus had been on putting out the fire before something really bad happened, and he'd forgotten to think about himself.

He started to massage it, winced, and slipped it back into the sling. With any luck, it would continue to mend, and he could start light duty next week. Eight hours a day, five days a week, doing filing and other administrative work. Not his job of choice. He preferred working a pair of back-to-back, twenty-four-hour shifts, fighting fires, or serving as a paramedic. Still, light duty beat sitting at home, twiddling his thumbs, and trying to study. The two weeks he'd just suffered through was more than enough time off.

"When did you last have a fire and life safety training refresher?" he asked Rosemary.

"I'm not sure. Maybe a year? Do you remember, José?"

"I'd say more like two."

This year, Nate was in charge of safety training, and Adam made a mental note to let him know to schedule something here. For all he knew, Nate might be on the engine today. Since Adam had been forced to take disability leave, he'd lost track of who did what this month.

"Let's clean up this mess and get back to work," Rosemary said.

José nodded. "I'll toss everything I was cooking, and start over."

"I'll let our customers know," Rosemary said. "Adam, how about coffee and a treat on the house?"

He couldn't argue with that. "A scone and an espresso sound good. Make it a double. I need the extra caffeine. This studying is a real bear."

Rosemary frowned. "What are you studying for?"

"The exam I need to pass so I can get promoted to lieutenant." That was the next rung up from senior firefighter and one rank below captain. Adam already knew a lot of what he needed for the job, but the class he'd enrolled in focused on management skills, which he didn't have. He'd made it more than halfway through the sixteen-week course, but there was still a lot to learn before the written test in late February. The class and the studying were rougher than he'd expected.

He returned to the restaurant and watched the diners file inside again.

In the midst of that, Rafe, Daniel, Hank, and Max strode in, just as Adam had known they would. Big men, decked out in fire gear.

"Like I told you, it's been handled," Adam greeted them.

"You know the drill," Adam's best bud, Rafe, replied.

Adam's crewmates tromped into the kitchen to

make sure the fire was out and check for fire within the walls.

Samantha and her kid returned to their booth. She handed him his backpack.

"Mind if join you?" Adam asked.

When the little guy grinned, she shrugged. "Okay.

Adam slid in beside him, putting him across from Samantha. He'd heard about her—divorced, moved to Guff's Lake six months ago, house-sitting Lucy Marks's place while the older woman wintered in Palm Desert.

She was a looker—short black hair, long, wispy bangs, big eyes, and a sexy mouth that made him think of pleasure. But he didn't get involved with single mothers. He never had, mainly because most of them were looking for husbands. And judging by the relationships Adam had screwed up, he figured he'd make a lousy husband and father.

"Was it a big fire?" the boy asked. He had his mother's eyes.

"It could have been," Adam said. "But it's all good now."

William nodded somberly. "What happened to your arm and leg?"

Adam shrugged. "I hurt them fighting a fire." With his wrist still screaming, he figured he'd set himself back. That really teed him off, and not only because he wanted back on regular duty. Until he healed, he couldn't take the physical exam he needed to qualify for lieutenant.

Between the management class, the written and physical exams, and the interview, the whole process would take roughly four months. Time he couldn't afford to make up later, not if he wanted his father to see him promoted.

To finally make him proud. Adam wanted that just about more than he'd ever wanted anything.

His buds returned to the restaurant, stopping at the booth where Adam sat.

Every one of them looked Samantha over.

"Hello. I'm Rafe Donato." Flashing the twin dimples that had women falling all over him, Rafe shook her hand.

"This is Samantha and her son, William," Adam said by way of introduction. "I just met them myself. Samantha makes all that stuff in the front case."

"So you're the talent behind those scones. I'm Max Meier."

Max also shook her hand. Women said his brown eyes were soulful, and Samantha looked as if she bought that hook, line, and sinker.

Adam didn't like it, but what did he care? "These two other guys are Daniel and Hank."

Lanky Daniel grinned, and Hank, the station's newest and most solemn firefighter, nodded.

Each of them shook hands with her kid, who was all eyes.

Other diners came over to say hello. Adam didn't miss the looks women gave him and his buds. They were used to that.

A moment later, Rafe checked his watch. "We're a little over an hour until the end of our second shift. We should go."

The crew's back-to-back shifts started at eight

a.m. on Mondays and ended at eight a.m. on Wednesdays, when another crew took over.

"Good to meet you, William. Samantha." Rafe nodded to Rosemary and the waitresses. "I'll see you ladies for breakfast shortly."

As they filed out, Adam swore he heard collective female sighs.

Although Samantha seemed immune to his crewmates' charms. Adam wasn't about to examine why he felt relieved.

"We should leave now, too," Samantha said. "We still have another delivery to make, and then William needs to get ready for school."

Already standing, the boy cupped his groin and danced from foot to foot. "Mom, I gotta pee."

Samantha gave Adam a Kids, what can you do? look and then slid quickly from the booth. "Hurry, before you have an accident."

"I don't wanna use the girls' bathroom."

"Well, I can't go into the men's."

"I'll take him," Adam offered.

Unsure whether she should trust this man she'd just met with her son, Samantha hesitated. "That isn't necessary."

"I gotta go right now," William insisted.

"He's a good guy," Janna added from a nearby table, where she was pouring coffee.

Samantha relaxed. Anyway, there was no time to argue. Adam ferried her son toward the men's room. "Sit tight, Sam," he said over his shoulder. "We'll be right back."

Sam. Adam had called her Sam. Samantha sat back in the booth and sighed. She didn't go by the shortened version of her name anymore, hadn't since high school. Even her parents called her Samantha.

She kind of liked hearing it again on Adam's lips. Not that she was interested in him. She wasn't, she assured herself.

By the time he brought her son back, she was up and waiting with her coat on and holding out William's.

"Thanks, Adam." She helped her son into his parka.

"No prob. Be good, sport."

"I will."

"Hey, I'll be back at work next week. If you ever want to visit the fire station, give me a call and I'll show you two around." Adam wrote his cell number on the back of his card.

"Really?" William looked as if it was Christmas morning.

Samantha preferred to steer clear of the firefighter she was attracted to, but she couldn't bear to disappoint her son. "We just might take you up on that."

A tour to please William, and that would be that. As they headed toward the car, she pushed the firefighter from her thoughts.

ALSO BY ANN ROTH

Ann Roth Classics

A Place to Belong

Father of the Year

Another Life

My Sisters

Dunlin Shores

Book 1 Just the Way You Are

Book 2 Wedding Bell Blues

Book 3 Falling for Mr. Wrong

Book 4: A Special Kind of Love

Firefighters

Book 1 Mr. January

Book 2 Mr. February

Book 3 Mr. March

Book 4: Mr. April

Book 5: Mr. May

Book 6: Mr. June

Book 7: Mr. July

Book 8: Mr. August

Book 9: Mr. September

Book 10: Mr. December

www.ingramcontent.com/pod-product-compliance
Lightning Source LLC
Chambersburg PA
CBHW010543100726
47903CB00011B/3124

9781648395345

ABOUT THE AUTHOR

Ann Roth is an award-winning author of 40-plus contemporary romance and women's fiction novels, as well as novellas and numerous short stories. Her first novel was published in 2000 by Harlequin Special Edition and was nominated by *Romantic Times* as best first book. Ann lives with the love of her life in the Greater Seattle area and enjoys creating flawed characters and putting them in challenging situations that help them grow and ultimately find love— whether or not they're looking for it.

Find out about new releases!
Sign up for my newsletter

Or visit my website www.annroth.net